The Group - Week Two

M. D. MEYER

LEWIS

Copyright © 2011 M. D. Meyer

All rights reserved. Neither this publication nor any part of this publication may be reproduced or transmitted in any form or by any means, electronic or mechanical, including photocopying, recording or any information storage and retrieval system, without permission in writing from the author.

"Take My Hand" by Jean–Luc Lajoie. Copyright 1994 by Malaco Music Co./Le Kri Music, Inc./Peermusic 111, Ltd. International Copyright secured. Used by permission. All rights reserved.

Material from pages 153–156 from *Helping Victims of Sexual Abuse* used by permission. Copyright 1989 by Bethany House Publishers, a division of Baker Publishing Group. *Helping Victims of Sexual Abuse* was written by Lynn Heitritter and Jeanette Vought. All rights reserved.

This is a work of fiction. Names, characters, places and incidents either are the product of the author's imagination or are used fictitiously, and any resemblance to actual persons, living or dead, businesses, companies, events, or locales is entirely coincidental.

ISBN: 978–1–77069–262–6

Printed in Canada.

Word Alive Press
131 Cordite Road, Winnipeg, MB R3W 1S1
www.wordalivepress.ca

Library and Archives Canada Cataloguing in Publication

Meyer, M. D. (Mary Dorene), 1957-
    Lewis / M.D. Meyer.

(The group ; week 2)
ISBN 978-1-77069-262-6

    I. Title. II. Series: Meyer, M. D. (Mary Dorene), 1957- Group ; week 2.

PS8626.E933L49 2011   C813'.6   C2011-900962-5

"I could walk a thousand miles to find hope..."

Robert Quill
Pikangikum, 2002

"WE NEED TO TELL OUR STORY to a trustworthy friend or counselor. As we tell our story, we are in touch with the pain and shame we experienced as a child.

"God wants to express His love for us in a tangible way. Often it is through the eyes, hugs and words of a friend."

> Howard Jolly
> Moose Factory, 1996

Chapter 1

"I meant you, Injun!"

Lewis stood his ground. There were two of them. The one who'd spoken looked to be about his height and weight but the other was a couple of inches taller and about a hundred pounds heavier.

The smaller one smirked. "Maybe you don't speak English."

Lewis didn't move. He was prepared to fight to protect her if he had to. He couldn't see Starla but had a clear image of her huddled into the corner behind him, trembling from the cold—or perhaps in pain. He'd finally found her after hours of searching the city streets. He'd almost reached her. He'd been so close!

All he wanted to do now was take her into his arms—tell her that everything was going to be all right. He would take her back home away from all this. And no one would ever hurt her again!

But before he'd even had a chance to speak her name—to let her know that he was here now—these thugs had appeared out of nowhere and now he was standing in front of her, willing to defend her with his very life if he needed to. One of them was swinging a baseball bat, moving closer...

"Yeah, he speaks English all right."

Lewis whirled around. Starla!

She was trembling—with laughter!

Lewis

The bat struck his left leg and Lewis fell to his knees. The pain was excruciating.

Now all three of them were laughing at him.

Laughing and laughing...

No... Someone was crying!

Lewis startled fully awake, his heart beating like a jackhammer. *Karissa was crying!* Lewis groaned as he tried to get out of bed, the cramp in his leg making it difficult to move at all.

"It's all right. Daddy's here."

"Mommy—wan' Mommy!"

Lewis lifted Karissa up out of her crib. "I do too," he whispered, pulling the little girl close, feeling her wet tears on his neck and shoulder. "I want her, too."

Lewis eased back down onto the mattress, thankful that there wasn't too much distance between his bed and her crib. It would have been difficult to move a whole lot further with his leg still cramping.

He pulled the covers up over both of them. Karissa was already falling asleep again, the tears from her cheeks soaking through the front of Lewis's sleeveless white t–shirt.

As the little girl slept on his chest, Lewis wondered if it was possible that Karissa had been dreaming about her mother at the same time that he himself had been dreaming about her.

Starla... It'd been over a month now since she'd left him— this time. Eighteen–month–old Karissa was just beginning to say a few words. Lewis hadn't even minded that she'd learned to say "Mommy" first and hadn't yet said "Daddy."

He had thought his wife had been home to stay.

Everyone had thought she was doing so much better. She had

seemed content to stay in Rabbit Lake—content to stay with him. As the weeks had stretched into months, through the fall and into the winter, Lewis had worried less and less about her leaving, and had focused more on renovating their home. He'd gutted the old bathroom, installing a full–size tub to replace the old shower stall and he'd built shelves and a cabinet to match the new sink. In the kitchen, he'd installed new cupboards and he'd hand–built a beautiful oak table for Starla, carving intertwined flowers, leaves and stems across its surface. He'd also made a crib for Karissa, a toy box and a little rocking chair.

The new bathroom had been expensive and transporting the wood had been costly. Even though they were less than a hundred air miles from the nearest full size lumber store, the only other ways in or out of Rabbit Lake were by boat in the summer and ice road in the winter. Fortunately, Lewis had been working steady since they'd got married, first at the Public Works department and then for the past eight months at Goldrock Camp. Lewis mostly did maintenance there but when they'd been running the youth program for troubled teens during the winter, he'd also had an opportunity to mentor some of the young people, teaching them carpentry and other woodworking skills.

Starla had gone each day to Goldrock Camp as well but she had been more of a participant than a staff member. The program was able to accommodate young mothers with children and Karissa was with her most of the day as Starla took classes in child–care and in cooking. Since she'd been gone so often throughout her teen years, Starla hadn't graduated from high school yet. At Goldrock Camp, she'd begun Grade 10 English and Grade 11 Math via the Internet but had left before finishing either of them.

Now, even though Starla was gone, Lewis often still brought

Karissa up to Goldrock Camp where the camp director's wife, Missy Quill, cared for her while Lewis worked. Randi, Lewis's sister–in–law, also babysat whenever Lewis asked, insisting that her nine–month–old son, Chance, played so well with Karissa that it was actually easier for her to take care of the two children than to spend all her efforts trying to keep Chance happy and busy.

Many others also offered their help and support just as they had the other time that Starla had left him. People brought meals over or sometimes just a loaf of homemade bread or some freshly baked cookies.

Lewis actually felt overwhelmed sometimes by all the help and attention. He was around people all day and often, in the evening, after Karissa was in bed, Lewis just wished that he could be alone with his thoughts.

But invariably, someone would stop over, put on a pot of coffee or tea and sit around visiting. Often, they came as a couple and the wife would watch Karissa while her husband talked Lewis into going to the gym to shoot a few hoops or when the ice had been solider, for an informal game of hockey.

And on Sundays, there was the support of the people in his local church. The morning services focused more on Bible teaching but the evenings were set aside for music. Lewis enjoyed playing up on the stage with the band. He'd been practicing on the drums there ever since he was little. Over the years, Kenny, the regular drummer had given him tips on how to improve and occasionally had let him take his place for a song or two. When Kenny had moved away from Rabbit Lake two years ago, Lewis had been invited to be the band's permanent drummer.

Now just about every day, Lewis would bundle up Karissa and walk the quarter mile or so to the church. Karissa was always content to play with a few toys on the stage while Lewis practiced on the drum set.

But though his days and evenings were filled, the nights often seemed to stretch on forever. Especially after he'd had one of his dreams—of her.

Lewis sighed, gently lifted Karissa off his chest and laid her beside him. He got out of bed slowly, careful not to wake her up yet. The morning went a little smoother if he had a head start on things, getting himself dressed and breakfast ready before Karissa woke.

He liked to have the house nice and warm for her, too. The fire from the night before wasn't quite out and Lewis was able to build it up easily with a few pieces of wood that he kept stacked in the enclosed porch built around his outside door. After he'd stoked the fire, Lewis moved around the cabin, opening the curtains on the four small windows, two that looked over the lake and one on either end of the large front room. It was a sunny but cold spring morning. At least it was spring according to the calendar—in two days, it would be Easter Sunday. But with the ice still on the lake and muddy slush covering the ground, it felt more like winter.

At least it was sunny today, Lewis mused. So often in the spring, it was cloudy and the whole world seemed as if it was dead or dying, cast in a dark gray shroud, nothing moving in the silence.

Lewis shook his thoughts free. The ice would melt. The birds would come back. The trees would bud. And for today at least, the sun was shining and he needed to think of his daughter—and breakfast—and the day ahead. Hopefully, Joshua had some physical work that needed to be done at the camp today. Something like hammering nails or chopping wood...

Lewis pulled a carton of eggs out of the refrigerator and grabbed the loaf of seven-grain bread from the cupboard. He rarely felt hungry anymore but always forced himself to make nutritious meals for Karissa's sake. They usually ate lunch at the camp and were often invited to stay for supper as well, but breakfast was always Lewis's responsibility.

This morning he scrambled some eggs and made toast before going to get his daughter. Karissa was easy to wake up and always seemed ravenously hungry the very moment her eyes opened—a typical morning person.

As Lewis set Karissa down into her high chair, she gave him a big toothy grin. And when he sat down to join her for breakfast, she began babbling away to him in baby talk. Lewis couldn't understand a lot of what she was saying but when Karissa needed him to do something for her, she managed to somehow communicate it to him. If they were walking and she was tired, she'd say "Uppie" and Lewis would pick her up. When they were at the lodge at Goldrock Camp and she was ready to go home, she'd say, "Bye–bye." And she certainly knew how to say no if there was ever anything she didn't like.

Karissa seemed to be enjoying her breakfast this morning. She could pretty much feed herself. She had a sippy cup for her milk and Lewis cut up her toast and banana into small pieces that were easy for her to pick up. He encouraged Karissa to use a spoon for softer food but she still preferred her fingers for most things. Both her and Lewis liked Ketchup with their scrambled eggs and jam on their toast and often Karissa would get Lewis's attention by patting him on the arm and there would usually be either ketchup or jam or something on her hand that would end up getting transferred to Lewis's arm.

And, of course, some of Karissa's food would fall on the floor. Usually, by the time breakfast was over, there was sticky goo all over Karissa's chubby baby cheeks, her downy baby curls, her hands, her clothes, her highchair, the floor and usually all over Lewis as well!

Most of the time, it was just easier to dunk the little girl into a tub of water for her morning bath than to try to get her clean with a washcloth. She still wore a diaper at night but had Pull–Ups during the day. She was doing well with her potty training but often still wet her diaper at night—especially if she'd had a bad dream and woke up crying like she had the night before.

Karissa loved bath–time. She had some plastic boats that she liked to play with in the water and she would happily stay in the tub as long as Lewis allowed her.

He had a small portable radio on a special shelf that he'd built in the bathroom and this morning, as usual, he turned the radio on to listen to the news while he brushed his teeth and combed his hair, all the while keeping an eye on Karissa splashing in the tub.

She seemed to be spending most of her efforts trying to sink the little toy boats and would giggle every time when they popped back up again. Lewis hoped that he would be able to take his daughter for a real boat ride in the summer. Keegan had said that he would like to spend more time out on the lake this year and he'd promised to bring Lewis and Karissa with him.

"Well, I think it's time you got out," Lewis said, bending over to pick up the little girl. "We need to get ready to go."

But Karissa had other ideas. She began to kick and scream. "No! No go! Wan baff!"

Lewis found himself struggling to keep hold of the slippery little child who was working her way up to a full–sized temper tantrum.

His new shirt was soaking wet by the time Lewis finally hauled

Karissa out of the tub, screaming now at the top of her lungs.

He wrapped her in a towel and carried her out of the bathroom—only to come face to face with his boss, Joshua Quill.

In contrast to Lewis's disheveled appearance, Joshua looked like he'd just stepped off the cover of a magazine. They were similar enough in physical appearance to be brothers, both with jet–black hair and dark brown eyes, slim build and average height but for some reason that Lewis couldn't fathom, Joshua always seemed to effortlessly have more style, more confidence.

Even though he likely wasn't going anywhere special, Joshua had on a camel–colored, short–sleeve button down shirt and charcoal gray pants. Lewis had his typical faded blue jeans with the inevitable small but irremovable wood stain splashes. He normally chose his t–shirts in dark colors so lingering stains wouldn't show up. Well, he was a working man—and a father.

Karissa was still crying, great hiccupping sobs now with huge tears running down her cheeks.

"Can I help?" Joshua offered, stretching his arms out to Karissa but speaking to Lewis.

"She just didn't want to get out of the bath." Lewis couldn't help but feel a little anoyed. *He was a good father. Why did Joshua have to see him like this?*

"Am I late or something?" Lewis mumbled.

"No," Joshua answered as Lewis let him take Karissa. "You don't have to rush to get over there—especially now when we're taking a break between students." Joshua sat down with Karissa on his lap still wrapped up in a large towel. He pulled his Swiss Army knife out of his pocket and handed it to her and the tears stopped as suddenly as if a tap had been shut off.

Lewis stared at them. "Isn't that dangerous?" he asked.

"Nah, she can't get it open," Joshua said, watching as Karissa carefully examined the bright red object. Joshua looked up suddenly. "But if you'd rather she didn't have it…"

Lewis slumped down into a chair beside them. "No, it's okay," he said wearily. "At least she's quiet now."

Joshua looked thoughtful. "You know you don't need to rush over in the mornings," he said again. "Family is important, too."

At age twenty-four, Joshua Quill was just five years older than Lewis but, perhaps because of his position as owner and director of Goldrock Lodge *and* Lewis's position as worker there, Joshua was usually the one to dispense advice.

But Lewis hadn't slept at all after he'd woken up from the nightmare—and it just seemed way too early in the morning for a lecture!

He pulled Karissa off Joshua's lap. The knife fell and the little girl began to cry, "Wanna, wanna…"

Lewis shifted Karissa from two arms to one and bent to pick up the knife, not breaking stride as he moved towards the bedroom. He laid her on the bed, silencing her cries by putting the knife back in her hand as he got a Pull-Ups out of the box beside her crib and slipped them on her.

"The reason that I came over…" Joshua spoke from the doorway.

Lewis ignored him as he struggled now to put socks on the little girl's kicking feet.

"You left your cell phone up at the lodge yesterday," Joshua said, dropping the phone down on the bed.

Karissa immediately made a lunge for it. Lewis picked it up and put it on the bedside table. Karissa began to cry again, "Wanna, wanna…"

Lewis handed her the Swiss Army knife and shoved one of her legs into the size 2 pants that he'd bought at the Northern Store just the past week. It was the first time she'd worn them. They looked like they fit. Karissa was going to be tall like her mom.

The little girl began to use Joshua's knife as a drumstick, beating rhythmically on Lewis's head, all the while chanting, "Da, Da, Da, Da…"

Lewis sighed and took away the knife, knowing that Karissa would start to fuss again.

He wished Joshua would just leave. He'd given him the phone. Why was he still hanging around? Couldn't he see that they weren't having the greatest morning of their lives?

Lewis pulled Karissa onto his lap. Putting her shirt on was always the hardest part because Karissa didn't like the feeling of not being able to see, even if it was just for a second or two. She usually fought with Lewis and made it an even longer time.

Sure enough, she began to struggle as soon as Lewis tried to pull the shirt over her head.

"Can I—make a suggestion?" Joshua asked in a hesitant voice.

Lewis wanted to make a suggestion that he leave! Why did he think he knew so much about parenting anyway? He didn't even have a kid yet!

"What!" he demanded.

Joshua's quiet voice and calm manner were in sharp contrast to Lewis's rising frustration. Karissa responded immediately to his gentle voice as Joshua spoke her name, took the shirt from Lewis and held it up for Karissa to see.

"You can make it a game," Joshua said, sitting down beside them.

He held the shirt in front of her eyes, moved it away and said,

"Boo!"

The little girl giggled as Joshua repeated the process again and yet again.

Lewis couldn't help but be touched by the sound of unrestrained joy. Karissa's laughter filled the room and Lewis felt his own heart responding with a burst of happiness.

When Joshua stopped, Karissa cried out, "D'ain, d'ain!"

Joshua handed Lewis the shirt and said, "Daddy can do it this time."

Lewis felt a brief moment of panic. Karissa's lip was starting to quiver already. She was still on Lewis's lap and was looking fearfully up at the shirt, waiting as if for the axe to fall.

Lewis held the shirt up over his eyes. Then he lowered it, looked down at Karissa and did his best imitation of Joshua's, "Boo!"

The effect was dramatic and immediate. The little girl's eyes lit up and a huge smile covered her face. "D'ain, Daddy, d'ain!"

Lewis felt his heart soar. Karissa had called him, "Daddy!"

"She called me Daddy!" Lewis exclaimed.

Joshua laughed. "Yeah, I heard."

"You called me Daddy!" Lewis declared again, the shirt falling from his hands as he lifted the little girl high into the air.

"Pretend to be an airplane," Joshua suggested.

"An airplane!" Lewis began to whirl Karissa around above his head. "Brmmm, the airplane is flying high in the sky! Now it's flying all over Rabbit Lake. It's going to come down for a landing…"

They tumbled down onto the bed together, both of them laughing.

It felt strange hearing it from his own lips. He'd heard other people laugh. But this was different—and it felt good.

"D'ain, Daddy, d'ain!"

Lewis laughed again, marveling once more at the spontaneity of joy he was feeling. He'd smiled before. He'd even made some small sound in his throat in response to a joke. But this…!

Lewis lifted the little girl up again. "Karissa is flying through the sky, flying and flying! Out to the kitchen, zooming by Joshua…"

Joshua smiled and waved at them as they "flew" by.

Lewis's arms grew tired and once more he made a not so smooth landing, tumbling down onto the bed in a wreath of laughter. Karissa fell in a giggling heap beside him. "D'ain, Daddy, d'ain."

"Easy for you to say!" Lewis declared. "You're not the engine, pilot, copilot, and cabin crew!"

"D'ain, Daddy, d'ain," Karissa insisted.

Lewis let his arms flop backwards onto the bed and closed his eyes. "Daddy's tired. Daddy's going to sleep."

Karissa giggled even more than she had with the airplane game.

Lewis opened one eye and smiled mischievously. Karissa jumped on top of him but immediately climbed off again as she felt Lewis's cold, wet shirt.

Lewis rolled over. "Hmm, so you don't like my wet shirt, eh?" He poked Karissa playfully in her tummy. "Well, you were the one who got it all wet!" He sat up again, found one of Karissa's favorite shirts, with a big red appliquéd puppy on it, and said, "I think we should both put on dry clothes. Here, you take yours." Lewis stood up to open his dresser drawer and was surprised to hear Joshua speak his name. He'd almost forgotten that he was there!

"The reason that I came here…"

Lewis dug a clean shirt out of his drawer, spied his cell phone and picked it up. "Yeah, thanks," he said, slipping his cell phone into his pocket. He took off his wet shirt, threw it over the side of the crib and pulled the dry one over his head.

"Not just that…"

There was something in the tone of Joshua's voice that caught and held Lewis's attention.

"You had a call on your cell phone last night."

Lewis eased down onto the bed.

"Starla…" he whispered.

Chapter 2

Joshua sat down beside him and pulled Karissa onto his lap. "We think it might have been her," he said gently. "Missy had gotten up in the night to get a drink. Otherwise, we probably wouldn't have heard it at all. You'd left your phone on the kitchen table."

Lewis groaned. The one time that he'd left his phone there! How many nights had he gone to sleep with it on the pillow beside him, afraid that he might miss her call? Now, the *one time* he'd forgotten…

Joshua continued. "The voice was so slurred that it was hard to even tell who it was—but Missy thought it sounded like Starla—and she was asking for you. Missy told her that you had left your cell phone at the lodge and suggested that she call you on your home phone. The person hung up before saying whether she would or wouldn't call you at home." Joshua paused. "I guess she didn't?"

Lewis shook his head.

Joshua sighed. "Missy felt so bad about it. She thought afterwards that she should have asked the person for her number right away…"

Lewis grabbed his cell phone and pressed a couple of buttons.

Joshua guessed what he was doing. "We already tried that."

Lewis read the message. "Number of last caller unknown."

He bowed his head. A tear splashed onto his cell phone. Lewis quickly raised his head and swiped at his eyes.

Joshua was still holding Karissa but now she had her shirt on! Joshua must have put it on her. But there'd been no crying—no struggle.

Lewis turned away. What was the use of even trying? He was a lousy father and a lousy husband.

He looked down at the cell phone again and his eyes blurred. She'd needed him—*and he hadn't been there for her!*

"Maybe she'll call again," Joshua suggested.

And maybe she won't!

"D'ain Daddy," Karissa spoke hesitantly, sensing as children do, that something was wrong but not understanding how to deal with it.

Lewis couldn't imagine playing a game right now. He couldn't imagine laughing when Starla was—

But that was just it. *He didn't know how she was doing or even where she was!* He never did know when she went away like this. She'd just disappear one day and people would say that they'd seen her get on a plane—or they'd seen her on a bus…

"Missy and I could take Karissa for the morning—if you need a bit of time," Joshua suggested.

You can take her forever! Lewis turned his back on the sight of Karissa sitting contentedly on Joshua's lap and walked out of the room.

It was just like his father had always said. He was good for nothing. Some days Lewis thought he had proved his father wrong. He was good at carpentry. He was good at music. But at the things in life that really counted—his relationships with other people—his father was right. "Aan enaabadiziyin?" his father would ask the rhetorical question in Ojibway, emphasizing the words. *What are you good for?*

Nothing, I'm good for nothing. I'm good at nothing. I am nothing.

Joshua walked out of the bedroom, chatting cheerily to Karissa about going for a truck ride and going to see Missy.

Lewis watched in silence as Joshua put the little girl's coat and boots on.

Joshua was going to make a great father. His wife was two and a half months pregnant. Soon they'd have their own child to take care of.

Joshua had said they would watch Karissa for him. Give him time…

Time! What would he do with time?

As Joshua stood hesitantly by the door, Karissa in his arms, Lewis finally found his voice. "I—I was thinking you might have some outdoor work for me to do today. Maybe, something like chopping wood or shoveling snow…"

Joshua nodded and led the way to his truck. They had been driving for a few minutes when he began in a slow thoughtful voice, "I am a little worried about the roofs of some of our cabins. They're old and there's quite a bit of heavy wet snow on them. It probably wouldn't be good to wait the whole weekend to get them cleaned off."

He'd made it sound as if the job was urgent—and Lewis was grateful. Shoveling off the roofs would be just the kind of hard, physical work that Lewis needed to relieve the tension that had been steadily building up in him ever since his dream the night before.

They rounded the last corner and the camp came into view. Originally the site of a gold mine, many of the old buildings were still in place, including the tall head frame that could be seen for many miles around. Goldrock Lodge and the five cabins on the property had been built by a wealthy former basketball player, Tom Peters, and less than a year ago, willed by Tom to Joshua Quill.

The lodge itself was beautiful inside and out with huge windows facing the lake fronting a dining room that rose two stories to a soaring cathedral ceiling with sparkling chandeliers and a sloping roof with large skylights.

The back part of the building had three bedrooms and a bathroom upstairs, and a bedroom with an adjoining bathroom downstairs adjacent to the large, well—equipped kitchen. The front dining room had two lounge areas, one on either end. The south wall had a huge stone fireplace that was nice on cool evenings but inadequate in itself to heat the lodge. Instead, there was a heat pump system that used the lake as a huge thermal reservoir heating the lodge in the winter and cooling it in the summer.

Lewis, interested in all types of building design, found working at Goldrock Camp to be a constant learning experience. With a natural aptitude for woodworking and with the availability of excellent tools and building supplies, Lewis was constantly at work trying new designs for cupboards, tables, chairs and even beds. And there were bigger projects too like replacing doors and windows on the old cabins or tearing down or building up new walls as needed. Lewis could order the books he needed to teach the young people in the program. He also ordered books for himself.

And he accessed the Internet as well, never afraid to use new techniques or improvise to make something more useful—or more beautiful. He felt the same flow of creativity with wood as he did with music and he felt no hesitation there either. When he was drumming, he was totally in sync with the music and could improvise even as he kept in time with the rest of the band.

But when it came to people, Lewis felt none of the courage he experienced with music and carpentry.

As they walked into the lodge, Lewis wasn't noticing any of the beautiful architecture. He was thinking about what he'd say to Joshua's wife, Missy. As she walked towards them, Lewis lowered his gaze, his thoughts all running together in confusion. Should he thank her for taking Starla's call?—Apologize that she'd had to answer his cell phone in the middle of the night?—Or just say nothing at all?

But Missy's thoughts were elsewhere. "Isn't it the most incredibly gorgeous day!" she exclaimed. "Just look at the way the sun shines through the chandeliers and sends rainbows all over the room!" She took Karissa into her arms and pointed upwards. "Look honey, look at the pretty colors."

Karissa made soft "oohing" sounds and her eyes shone as she and Missy gazed up at the ceiling together.

Lewis was reminded that Missy had been blind for most of her life, receiving her sight less than a year ago through a transplant operation. Now, she delighted in everything around her. She especially loved color, today dressed in purple pants and a bright floral print fuchsia top that set off the glow on her ebony skin. Like Joshua, she looked stylish but comfortable in whatever she was wearing. Her curly, black hair was tied back with a scarf that matched her silk top.

Lewis wondered if he had dressed Karissa well enough. Maybe he should have put on a new shirt as well as new jeans.

As if in answer to his thoughts, Missy gushed, "Lewis, you have the most absolute cutest little girl I've ever seen!"

Standing awkwardly on the front doormat not wanting to take

off and then put back on his boots, Lewis smiled his thanks to her.

"Lewis is going to shovel the snow off the roofs of our cabins today," Joshua said, exchanging his black leather dress boots for a pair of brown leather loafers. Again, Lewis felt out of "Joshua's league" as he gazed down at his scuffed but sturdy work boots. Most people he knew just went around their house in stocking feet but not Joshua. Lewis thought it was likely Missy's big city upbringing that had changed him. Or maybe it was the responsibilities of being the owner of Goldrock Lodge and starting the youth program…

"Bye–bye da–da!" Karissa called out as Lewis turned and reached for the doorknob.

Lewis turned to smile at his daughter. "Bye, sweetie," he said. "Daddy will be back in a little while, okay?"

"Daddy baa…?"

"In a little while," Lewis promised.

He worked his way from cabin to cabin, using the sturdy wooden ladder that he'd built the past winter. Though the temperature hovered only a degree or two above freezing, Lewis was sweating by the time he had shoveled off the first roof and was down to his t–shirt by the time he got to the third cabin. He kept up a steady pace but his mind was only half on the job at hand. He couldn't stop thinking about Starla.

He wondered why she'd called.

Was she going to ask him to come and get her?

Lewis threw a huge shovel–full of snow off the roof. It fell with a heavy splatting sound.

No, more likely, she was just drunk and wanted someone to talk to. Starla didn't drink much but on the rare occasion when she did, she'd go all the way, drinking until she finally passed out cold. Along the way, she'd get weepy and sentimental. Missy had said that Starla's speech had seemed slurred.

The last time Starla had left him, she had called only once during the whole seven months she was gone—and she'd been drunk when she called. She had cried and said that she wanted to come back but in the end she had refused to tell him where she was. It had been four long months later when she had appeared back on his doorstep…

Lewis slid his shovel across the roof and scooped up another load, lifted it up and sent it flying over the edge.

She'd be sleeping it off by now. It was unlikely that she would call again.

Still Lewis felt for his cell phone. He'd never leave it anywhere again!

"Hey man! Be careful. You just about dropped that snow right on top of my head!"

Lewis looked down at his brother, Keegan. He was dressed in his police uniform, his thick, raven black hair neatly combed in a regulation haircut. Keegan must have just come off duty, working night shift again.

"I didn't hear you," Lewis said. "Sorry."

"Yeah, you were shoveling like a crazy man. What's up?"

Keegan could always tell if something was bothering him. There was no point in trying to hide it.

"Starla called." As he said the words, Lewis suddenly felt all his strength leaving him. He sank down onto the roof, his shovel still in his hands.

"What'd she say?" Keegan asked quietly, his voice carrying well in the stillness of the cold, spring air.

"Missy answered it. She just asked for me and then hung up."

"She'll come back."

Lewis looked out over the bleak landscape. The sun had gone behind some clouds and everything looked gray—even the thin ice—"black ice" they called it.

"Sometimes," he said, "I think it might be better if she would just stay away and never call. We could get on with our lives." Lewis looked down at his brother. "Karissa was crying for her in the night." He gazed at the frozen lake again. "Maybe eventually, if she never came back, we could both forget her."

Keegan didn't say anything for a moment. Then in a voice that was surprisingly gentle, he said, "C'mon down."

Lewis picked up the shovel and started down the ladder. "I just gotta finish one more roof," he said. "Joshua's expecting me to get them all done today."

"Joshua's the one who sent me," Keegan replied.

Keegan, larger in build than Lewis, had a longer stride than his younger brother but he kept apace with him as they walked together towards the lodge. "Joshua said to tell you that if the shoveling wasn't helping, you should take a break and try out some of his fresh, homemade hot cross buns."

"*His* hot cross buns—you mean Missy's don't you?"

Keegan laughed. "No, this time I think Joshua is actually the one who made them."

It smelled like a bakery when they opened the door of the lodge. Joshua was carrying a plate of buns into the dining area from the kitchen. Karissa was walking beside him, her little hand in Joshua's bigger one.

"Switching jobs with Missy?" Keegan teased him.

Missy was already sitting at one of the tables, sipping on some kind of herbal tea. Joshua set Karissa up in a booster seat at the table beside her and set a bun down in front of the little girl before answering. "No," he said, "I could never do what she does half as well as she does it."

Missy smiled cheerily. "And I could never do what he does half as well as he does it."

Lewis shook his head in amazement as he sat down beside them. *Those two—they always seemed to have it together!*

But Keegan couldn't resist another jib. "Well, you're sure wearing the apron today!"

Lewis thought maybe his older brother was taking it too far.

But it was Missy, not Joshua, who took offense at his statement.

"It's not a dishonor for a man to help his wife in the kitchen," she declared emphatically. "As it happens, I was feeling sick this morning—from being pregnant—definitely a woman's role. When Joshua suggested we make something special for Good Friday, I just about threw something at him. But then he offered to make the hot cross buns himself—and I think he did a really good job!"

Everyone quickly agreed with her, Keegan included.

Lewis stood up to get some coffee. There was a big coffeemaker on the counter jutting out from the kitchen "window" and people usually just helped themselves to coffee throughout the day.

He brought his cup of coffee back and sat down again. The dining room tables were small but comfortable enough for them all to sit around when there was just a few of them.

Joshua picked up the conversation again after Lewis had sat down. "It does bring up an interesting point though," he said. "Sometimes, we get too hung up on what roles each of us take."

Lewis looked up with interest, completely unprepared for what Joshua would say next.

"I've been reading a book recently about the effects of child sexual abuse on boys," Joshua said.

Lewis looked quickly down again as Joshua continued. "It's more difficult for them in some ways to begin their healing, especially if the perpetrator was a woman. But even if it was a man, they can't really talk about how weak and vulnerable they felt—and still feel. It's not considered 'macho' to say that you were hurt and are still hurting. A 'real man' is not supposed to cry—for himself—or for others. He's supposed to be big and tough."

"Our dad was big and tough," Lewis said in a voice he didn't recognize as his own. He immediately ducked his head again. *What had made him say that? And in front of Missy and Joshua!*

To his further surprise, Keegan agreed with him and even said more about their dad. "He used to beat us up," Keegan said in a low, gruff voice. "I used to think it was something I'd done." He shook his head. "But then, I realized it didn't matter what I did. If I cried, he said I was a sissy. If I didn't cry, he'd say I was trying to be 'Mr. Tough Guy' and he'd hit me harder."

Lewis wished the floor would open up under them as Keegan continued. "It wasn't just me either. He used to hit Lewis—and our mom."

Lewis could hear the pain in his brother's voice as he continued, "If Mom didn't have supper ready, he'd call her lazy and want to know what she'd been doing all day. If she did have it ready, he'd say it was cold or had been in the oven too long and was dried out, or had been on top of the stove too long and was overcooked. Nothing she could ever do was right. He'd come home mad and he'd find some reason to beat her."

"One day," Keegan went on, "I realized that I was now just as big—and maybe even stronger—than my dad. I turned around and started hitting him back. And then I just couldn't stop. My mom was crying. Lewis was crying. My mom tried to stop me and I pushed her away. Lewis tried to help and I pushed him away, too. I was just crazy mad. Then my mother screamed that I'd hurt you and that you were bleeding…"

Lewis didn't look up, even though he knew his brother was speaking to him, now. But he did remember how Keegan had pushed him away. He'd fallen and hit his head against the old cook stove. The head wound had bled quite a bit.

"It was like I suddenly realized that I was my father," Keegan said. "I called the police—on myself. It was Colin who came over—him and old Sammy Rae. He was the Police Chief then."

Lewis remembered it all as if it was yesterday. It was one of the few very clear memories in his childhood because from that day on, his father had never raised a hand to any of them. And Colin had stuck like glue to Keegan after that, helping him to get connected with the Internet to finish his high school and helping him to stop taking drugs. Then Keegan decided to follow Colin Hill's example and become a police officer…

"That's when I decided to become a police officer," Keegan's voice echoed Lewis's thoughts. "Colin really helped me with that. He told me what courses I should take in high school and how to apply to the police academy. Sammy Rae was a great influence, too. He taught me things you couldn't learn in school—stuff like courage and integrity. I guess he was like a grandpa to me."

There was a brief moment of silence. Then Joshua spoke in a quiet voice. "I never really heard your story before," he said. "You know, that's what we're hoping people will do in our support group session this week. What would you feel about maybe leading out and sharing your story with the whole group when we meet together on Wednesday night?"

Lewis glanced up at his brother and was horrified when Keegan nodded silently.

Would they all have to share their "stories"? Maybe Keegan could speak for both of them. Lewis had always thought it was a blessing that he could remember so little of his early childhood. He sure didn't want to dredge it all up again! Especially the part where their mother had died…

"I know these support group meetings are difficult," Joshua said. "As part of our training to be facilitators, Missy and I attended a support group in Thunder Bay. It was difficult to share things with other people that we had never talked about to anyone at all ever before. But it was very healing for both of us."

"Yes," Missy agreed. "It helped me to understand Joshua better. How the things that had happened in his life—the sexual and physical abuse that he'd suffered—had affected him even now in our life together as husband and wife. I began to understand how difficult it was for him to make decisions because of his low self-esteem and how much he needed my support and encouragement in his leadership role." Missy smiled at Keegan. "You see, I do feel that Joshua and I have different roles to play in our marriage and in our work here at the camp. But neither one of us can afford to get too nit-picky about what those roles involve. I *could* check the oil on our truck but I don't really like to. And I don't usually like him messing about in my kitchen."

Joshua was fixing her with an amused grin. "But you do like these hot cross buns I made?"

"Yes," Missy admitted, "now that my stomach has settled a little."

"And Karissa seems to have enjoyed hers," Joshua added.

Lewis had to smile. The little girl was covered with sticky

sugar, but it didn't seem to bother her a bit. She was gleefully licking each finger in turn. "So much for the bath and clean clothes I put on her this morning," he said.

"I'll get a washcloth," Missy volunteered. But before she could move, Joshua put a hand on her shoulder. "It's okay, I'll get it."

Lewis felt a pang of jealousy. It must be so great to have a relationship like that. Even the times when Starla had been home, there hadn't been that kind of harmony between them. He wondered if there could ever be the trust relationship between them that he knew should be there. Maybe part of it was that he never had any warning as to when she was going to leave. It would seem as if everything was going well…

She had left him the first time just two days before Christmas—*Karissa's first Christmas!* This time she'd gone the day before her 18th birthday. And she'd even missed the big party her father had organized for her. Her dad had even bought a beautiful new dress for her from some big fancy store in the city.

Lewis sometimes wondered if it had something to do with holidays or celebrations. Starla did seem to get pretty stressed out at those times. This past Christmas she'd talked him into going to a hotel in Thunder Bay for three days. There was a swimming pool and it had been fun but Lewis had missed the celebrations in Rabbit Lake—and he hoped that she wouldn't want them to leave the community for Christmas this coming year.

But maybe Starla wouldn't even be here. Maybe she wouldn't be coming back at all this time. Maybe it would be better.

Lewis watched as Joshua helped Karissa down out of the booster seat. Karissa knew where the box of toys was kept and ran to it without a backwards glance.

Lewis touched his cell phone. Yes, he thought, maybe it would be better if she never called again. Their lives could go on. They would get used to being without her.

His fingers closed around the cell phone. *If only he could hear her voice just one more time though…*

It was as if his thoughts had traveled across space and time.

The cell phone rang.

Chapter 3

It was Starla!

Her voice wasn't slurred but she sounded as if she was sick or something. *Probably a hangover.*

But she sounded scared, too. "Come and get me—Lewis—please—come and get me."

He felt his throat constrict and he could barely speak. "Where?" he finally managed in a hoarse whisper.

"I'm in jail."

"Tell me where exactly?" Lewis asked, frantically motioning for a pen and paper from those still gathered around the table. Keegan pulled a small notebook from the pocket of his uniform. A pen was clipped onto it.

Lewis heard Starla ask "where?" and suddenly another voice was on the line. The directions were given to Lewis in a brisk, official manner followed immediately by the question: *"How soon can we expect you?"*

Lewis once more sent a frantic look around the table. "I need to go to Winnipeg," he said.

"Excuse me sir, could you repeat that?"

"We'll go with you," Joshua said quickly.

"Can you come and get her or not?"

"Yes," Lewis said decisively, his heart still in his throat.

"We appreciate your cooperation."

"Wait!" Lewis called. "I want to talk to—" But it was too late. The person on the other end had hung up.

Lewis looked around in disbelief.

He'd wanted her to call—*or had he?*

"She—she's in jail," he stammered.

"We'll go with you," Joshua repeated.

"Randi and I can take care of Karissa," Keegan volunteered. "We're a little short-staffed down at the station right now or I'd go with you."

"No, it's all right," Missy assured him. "Joshua and I can go."

"If you need money for bail…" Keegan began.

Bail! "No, no, I'm sure it'll be all right," Lewis said quickly.

Joshua was already over at the phone calling the airport.

"They're booked solid," Joshua reported. "Lots of people traveling 'cause it's a long weekend. We can get tickets back to Rabbit Lake tomorrow; just none out today."

"We could try Bill," Missy suggested.

She was referring to Bill Martin who owned a Cessna 172 Skyhawk and ran a small business, transporting cargo and occasionally people. Joshua nodded and picked up the phone again. After a few moments conversation, he rejoined the group at the table. "Bill's got a trip out this morning but he can take us this afternoon. We should be at the airport by two. He can only bring us as far as Ear Falls. He's got another flight later on today as well."

Everyone turned towards Lewis who nodded. "That'll be great. Thanks."

He wished they could leave sooner but was grateful to Bill Martin for fitting them into his busy flight schedule.

"We should book a couple of hotel rooms in Winnipeg, too," Missy said. "I can do that online if you want."

"Yeah, that'd be great, honey," Joshua said. "And I'll get us a flight back tomorrow."

Lewis listened as Joshua talked to the ticket agent again. "Yes, three tickets from Ear Falls to Rabbit Lake."

"Four," Lewis said in a voice that cracked with emotion. He cleared his throat and said in a louder clearer voice, "We need four."

Joshua quickly apologized and amended his request. All eyes were on Lewis again, eyes filled with pity.

He stood up quickly and walked over to where Karissa was playing.

She looked up at him and her round face broke into a joyous grin of welcome. Lewis sat down beside her and focused all his attention on his daughter.

After a while, Keegan came over to join them, choosing a straight back chair to sit on. "I called Randi," he said. "She'll take care of Karissa while you're gone."

Lewis looked up at him. "Thanks."

"Joshua would like us to stay here overnight," Keegan continued.

Lewis nodded and turned his attention back to Karissa. He wasn't surprised that Joshua had asked them to "house–sit" the lodge. They'd helped out that way just the week before when Missy's sister, Jasmine, had been in the hospital and Joshua and Missy had gone down to Kenora to be with her.

"I think I'll head out now," Keegan said. "Can I give you a ride home?"

Lewis stood to his feet. "Yeah, that'd be good. I need to pack a few things."

Karissa fell asleep on the way and Lewis managed to carry her into the house without waking her up.

Once down for her nap, she was a pretty good sleeper so Lewis was able to move around the bedroom and pack a bag for her and another one for himself. He didn't need much—just a change of clothes, a toothbrush, toothpaste and comb. There was still room in the bag. Lewis wondered if he should pack anything for Starla. If she was in jail…

She hadn't taken much with her this last time—just his paycheck. But most of that would likely be gone now. She would have had to use some of it for the flight out…

Lewis had glanced briefly in Starla's dresser drawers once before when he'd put away bits of laundry she'd left. Now as he looked more carefully, he saw that her favorite jeans were still there. And a shirt that they'd bought in Thunder Bay last Christmas that he knew she liked to wear.

Lewis carefully packed them both into his bag. He continued to look through her drawers and on top of the dresser and in the bathroom, packing other little things that he thought she might want or need. In the kitchen, he took down a bag of green mints from off the top shelf. Starla was the only one who liked them but Lewis seemed to always end up buying some when he did his groceries each week—even now while she was away.

He sat down on the couch with the bag of mints in his hand, suddenly overcome with a deep sense of loss. He missed her. Pure and simple. He missed her.

He was still sitting there when Joshua arrived to pick them up, and Lewis had to wake up Karissa and take her to the potty and change her Pull–Ups. He was angry with himself that he hadn't thought about bringing her to the toilet before they'd left the lodge.

Karissa didn't like being rushed and was being cranky. Joshua was trying to be helpful, offering to take their bags out for them.

Lewis's frustration grew. Had he packed everything they needed? He put Karissa's extra mittens in the bag and wondered about sending a pair of shoes with her as well as her winter boots…

His eyes fell on Starla's running shoes. Maybe he should pack those too…

No, that was just crazy!

But if she was in jail, maybe she didn't have any clothes with her…

But she'd have shoes on her feet…

"Uh, Lewis, we need to go," Joshua spoke hesitantly.

Quickly adding the running shoes into his bag, Lewis grabbed an old jacket of hers and stuffed that in, too.

"Okay, that's it," he said, handing the two bags to Joshua.

As they pulled away from the house, Lewis glanced at his watch. It was just 1:35. They'd still make it in time.

But there were further delays at Randi and Keegan's because, for once, Karissa wasn't happy to be dropped off at her aunt and uncle's.

Lewis tried his best to comfort the little girl. "Daddy'll be back tomorrow…" he said, handing her over to Randi. But Karissa, perhaps picking up on his high anxiety level, seemed inconsolable. Lewis finally had to leave their house with her crying and reaching out for him.

They rushed to the airport and hurried across the tarmac towards the plane but when they reached it, they found Bill waiting patiently for them, seemingly in no hurry at all.

Lewis envied him his calm, easy–going temperament. Bill Martin ran his business well and he had a reputation for dependability. People could count on their cargo being transported safely, and his occasional passengers always enjoyed their ride. Bill had a friendly face to match his personality with a smile that came easily, sandy brown hair, blue–green eyes and a smattering of freckles across the bridge of his nose.

Any other time, Lewis would have been eager to be going for a ride with him. But he hated leaving Karissa the way he had. And he was worried about Starla…

There were some unexpected updrafts and the hour–long flight to Ear Falls turned out to be as turbulent as Lewis's emotions.

By the time they landed, Missy was feeling quite sick. Joshua helped her into the terminal and she spent quite a bit of time in the bathroom while they waited. Finally she emerged, looking only slightly better than when she'd gone in.

Joshua bought her a bottle of ginger ale to help calm her stomach. Lewis carried their bags as Joshua walked slowly with Missy across the parking lot to the van that was owned by Goldrock Camp and kept at the airport for when it was needed. Joshua got her settled into the front seat with a blanket and pillow and within minutes, Missy was fast asleep.

Joshua alternately played the radio or some CDs throughout the trip. Lewis was thankful that Joshua understood that he didn't feel like talking much. Even so, the five–hour trip seemed to last forever. They stopped briefly in Vermillion Bay for some coffee and again just outside of Winnipeg for gas and food. Joshua also bought a map and together he and Lewis found the location of the police station. By the time they got there, Lewis couldn't even wait for the van to come to a full stop. He rushed into the building and was looking around in desperation and growing despair when a police officer stepped forward and asked, "Is there something I can help you with, sir?"

"Starla—Starla Littledeer!"

"We're looking for a friend of ours," Joshua's calm voice sounded from behind him. "A young lady… She called us earlier today. She also called us last night. She sounded as if she might be a little intoxicated then. Maybe that's why she was here…?"

"Well, we get plenty of drunks this end of town, that's for sure." The police officer eyed them carefully. "Did you say you were family?"

"I am," Lewis spoke up. "She's my—my wife."

"Hmm… Well, let's have a look. I just came on duty myself. What did you say her name was?"

Lewis tried to speak clearly but his voice still shook a little as he said her name: "Starla Littledeer."

Joshua put a hand on Lewis's shoulder as the officer conferred with a colleague.

He came back to them a moment later with a piece of paper in his hand. "Apparently, there was a woman by that name here earlier today."

Lewis felt panic rising up like a giant wave threatening to pull him under.

"We had a report from a shop keeper that he had a vagrant outside on his doorstep this morning," the officer continued, his eyes still on the paper he was holding. "He said she appeared to be unconscious—possibly intoxicated. We sent a squad car round to pick her up. She was conscious and alert by the time they arrived. She passed the Breathalyzer test okay and seemed coherent enough. They considered bringing her to a hospital just as a precaution but she insisted that she was fine. They drove her back here but there wasn't really anything to hold her on. She asked to use the phone…"

The police officer read for a moment. "There was someone who was supposed to come and get her. He talked to one of our officers on duty."

"That was me," Lewis said in a hoarse voice. "Where is she?"

"I think they were expecting you right away…"

Joshua spoke up, apologizing for the delay and explaining about the distance that they'd had to travel.

"Where—where is she?" Lewis asked, trying once again to quell the rising panic that threatened to overwhelm him.

The officer looked vaguely around the room. "I'm not sure, actually." He conferred again with his colleagues but most of them hadn't been on the earlier shift and no one seemed to have noticed a young woman. "She must have left before any of us came on duty," the officer concluded.

"But where is she?" Lewis found himself asking yet again.

"Do you have any idea, sir, where she might have gone?" Joshua asked.

The officer shook his head. "Sorry, no idea. It's a big city. You would likely have a better idea than I would, seeing as how she's your friend…" His eyes swept past Missy and Joshua to met Lewis's. "…And your wife."

Lewis felt the words fall as a final judgment on him. He didn't know where his wife was. He hadn't known for the past month. *He should have known.*

"Let's go," Missy said gently.

Lewis made it to the van somehow. But he was finding it difficult to breath. And impossible to speak. Joshua drove the van into a side street and parked. Both he and Missy turned back, their eyes filled with concern.

"We'll find her," Joshua assured him.

Lewis shook his head and Missy reached back and took his hand. "It's going to be okay," she said.

Lewis took a deep shuddering breath. "I can't go through this again."

"We'll find her," Joshua said firmly. "If we have to turn the whole city upside down. We'll find her."

"And then what?" Lewis demanded breathlessly. "She's just playing games again. If she wanted me to take her home, she'd still be here."

"Maybe we should at least give her a chance to explain," Missy suggested. "Since we've come all this way…"

"…Again." Lewis finished the sentence for her. "I'm sorry to drag you through all this again. I should have just come back here alone."

"You didn't drag us," Joshua said gently. "We came with you because we wanted to."

Lewis shook his head. "I just need to forget her."

"You said you'd been through this before," Missy began in a puzzled voice. "Do you mean the police station here? Or coming to Winnipeg and not finding her…"

Lewis glanced up at Joshua, reluctant himself to tell the story.

"It was before we were married, honey—a couple of years ago, I guess," Joshua began hesitantly.

"Fifteen months," Lewis said sadly. He could recall to the day, every time she'd left him, every time she'd called…

"Starla was here in Winnipeg," Joshua continued in a heavy voice. "She called, begging Lewis to come down and get her. She was in jail—that time for real. Lewis paid her bail. She seemed really grateful—and maybe even glad to see us. But when we got outside the station, there were some people waiting in a car."

"Men…" Lewis mumbled, not looking up at either of them.

"Yeah, a couple of men," Joshua continued in a quiet voice. "She left with them."

"But who were they?" Missy asked. "Why did she go with them?"

"She never said," Lewis answered. "She just walked away from me without saying anything and went into their car. She didn't even look back as they drove away."

Lewis felt the crushing weight on his chest again, making it difficult to breath. "I should just forget her," he said hoarsely. "I—I don't think she even loves me—or her daughter."

No one spoke for a moment.

Joshua and Missy were still turned in their seats leaning towards him.

"We'll do whatever you want, Lewis," Joshua said. "If you want to just go to the hotel and head straight back tomorrow…"

Yes, he just wanted to go back home, to forget all about her.

"It's been a long day…" Joshua began.

"No!" Lewis groaned. He grabbed hold of Joshua's arm, feeling suddenly as though he were drowning. "Please help me find her—please."

"Are you sure that's what you want?" Missy asked.

Lewis turned desperate eyes on her. "No. I'm not sure about anything!"

"We'll look," Joshua said in a clear, decisive voice. He glanced down at his watch. "We'll give it till nine o'clock—and then we'll call it a night. And maybe," he added, "we can drive around for a bit in the morning again before we go."

Lewis nodded gratefully and Joshua and Missy turned back in their seats.

Joshua opened up the map again. "We should maybe look around this area first. And maybe mark the streets as we cover them." He handed the map to his wife. "Do you have a pen?" he asked.

As she dug one out of her purse, Joshua advised, "Lewis, if you could move over and look out the other window, you could cover the left hand side of the street. It'll be easier for Missy to navigate and watch the right hand side."

Lewis quickly complied. But any hopes they had of finding her right away, soon faded.

They finally took a break an hour later. Missy had to use the bathroom and Joshua wanted another coffee. They picked up a dozen donuts as well.

As they continued on their way, Lewis found he wanted to look at both sides of the street at once. But he did try to keep his main focus on the left hand side. He didn't want to chance missing her, especially as it got darker.

They were in an older section of town now. Joshua had the headlights on and as he was driving, his focus was further ahead than that of Missy or Lewis. And it was he who first noticed…

"Look there—in that alley!"

Lewis looked—and almost jumped out into traffic. "Wait!" Joshua yelled as Lewis yanked the van door open.

A car passed on their left. Joshua slowed to a stop on the narrow one–way street and called out, "We can't park here. I have to go around the block, I think."

Lewis didn't care what they did—as long as he could go to Starla.

He was sure it was her, his certainty growing as he closed the distance between them.

She was huddled on the steps of a side entrance of what looked like an old factory building. The long narrow alleyway behind her was dark but she'd been wearing a pale blue tube shirt and white jeans and these had enabled Joshua to spot her from the van. Her hair was covering her face but Lewis could see that she was still alive at least. She was trembling—probably from the cold.

He took it all in at once—the image of her printed indelibly on his mind. He unzipped his coat. She was cold…

It was as if the men had been waiting for him.

It was all happening again. They were the ones in his dream.

For an instant Lewis was paralyzed with fear. Then he jumped in front of her. He would protect her with his very life if necessary!

Suddenly, he recognized the faces. They weren't just from his dream. He'd seen them before. They were the ones who'd been waiting outside the jail that other time.

But only two of the three of them had been in his dream and Lewis knew instinctively that this third man was the one to be most feared. Standing, leaning on the opposite wall, his eyes hard and black as obsidian, long dark hair pulled back from his lean, angular face, he seemed to be biding his time, everything in his arrogant pose declaring that he alone was in total control.

The other two grabbed Lewis and held him while the third man took two long strides towards them. Raw hatred radiated from his being as he began to punch Lewis repeatedly in his upper body, the blows coming so hard and fast that Lewis was unable to catch his breath.

His two captors were unprepared for the sudden karate chop dealt to Lewis's shoulder, the force of the impact driving him to his knees. They both lurched forward but released their hold on Lewis before losing their balance.

The thinner man on the right swore and the bulkier one took a step forward, demanding, "Whatcha do that for?"

Lewis watched the pointed black boots move past him as a voice snarled, "Get outta my way, Denny."

Lewis tried to turn towards Starla but as he moved his head, the world began to spin, his stomach muscles contracted, and he was unable to stop himself from throwing up.

He heard the voice of his attacker speaking in a contemptuous snarl. "So this is what you left me for?"

Lewis saw the black boot coming towards him but was helpless to move out of the way as it made contact with his chest, knocking out what little breath he had left and sending him flying backwards onto the gravel.

The darkness began to close in and Lewis fought to stay conscious. From a distance, he heard the voice, changed now, speaking in a smooth and seductive tone. "You were one of my best girls, Starla. Sometimes you were even Number One."

Lewis strained to hear her reply but there was none.

"You could come back to me again, Starla. But you have to put this little Indian boy out of your mind once and for all."

Still there was no response from Starla.

Why wasn't she saying anything? What was she thinking? Was it so hard to make a decision? Why had she even called him!

"C'mon Starla, how could you want that pathetic little piece of trash? He can't even defend himself. How could he ever protect you?"

Lewis heard her cry out. He opened his eyes and saw that she was standing above him but her head was being forced back, a huge chunk of her thick black hair wrapped around the man's hand.

"Just remember, if you go with him now, you can never come

back. And there'll never be anyone to protect you. You'll be all alone!"

Suddenly Lewis heard voices calling his name and Starla's. *Finally!*

The two thugs melted away into the dark alley. Their leader let go of Starla's hair and she crumpled down on top of Lewis.

"Just remember," the voice hissed from out of the darkness, "you'll have *no one* to protect you now."

By the time Joshua and Missy reached them, Lewis and Starla were alone and the only sound was Starla's quiet sobbing.

Lewis could barely breathe, let alone speak and Joshua and Missy's loud exclamations and determined questions felt like an artillery bombardment.

Are you all right? What happened? We should call an ambulance. Or the police. Starla, what happened? Lewis, can you hear me?

Lewis found himself incapable of answering any of their questions. It was an effort just to keep his eyes open and focused on their faces.

But Starla had finally found her voice. "We've got to get out of here!" she cried frantically. "They might come back. Please, we've got to go!"

"He needs a doctor," Missy argued. "And we should call the police."

But Joshua had made his decision. "I'll go get the van."

Lewis heard his retreating footsteps, running hard on the concrete. He closed his eyes.

He could still hear Starla weeping.

Starla—his sometimes wife…

With a screech of tires, the van was back and suddenly they

were pulling him to his feet. Lewis's legs felt like rubber and he cried out in pain as they lifted his arms onto their shoulders and practically dragged him into the van and laid him down on the back bench seat.

Starla collapsed, out of Lewis's view, in one of the front-facing middle seats. He heard the door slam shut, heard Missy and Joshua get in; then the van began to move forward.

He wanted to talk to Starla but knew that he didn't have the strength to raise his voice. And what would he say?

He longed for her to turn back and speak to him. Just a word or two...

He could picture her in his mind. Her glossy black hair shimmering around her shoulders, her lovely smile that could light up a room, her flawless skin, her perfect teeth, her beautifully arched eyebrows and dark lashes gracing eyes that were the color of dark chocolate...

Lewis winced as the bright interior light came on again. A moment later, Joshua was leaning over him. "I hope we did the right thing moving you," he said in a worried voice. "It's not what I would normally do."

Lewis kept his eyes open but didn't try to speak.

"We're at a hospital. I'm going to see if I can get a wheelchair for you."

Joshua had barely left when another light was shone through the van and knuckles rapped sharply on Missy's window. "You'll have to move this car, ma'am," an authoritative voice spoke.

"My husband just went in to get a wheelchair," Missy explained.

"You'll need to move the van. This is for emergency vehicles only," the man insisted.

Lewis heard Missy sigh and get out of the vehicle.

She was in the driver's seat when Lewis returned, an exasperated tone in his voice. "They say there's none available."

"I have to move the van," Missy told him.

"Let me get Lewis out first," Joshua insisted. "Starla, you help me."

Chapter 4

SHE DIDN'T HAVE THE STRENGTH to move, never mind help someone else!

"C'mon, Starla, hurry up," Missy said irritably. "That security guard's coming back. You want Lewis to have to walk all the way from the parking lot?"

Joshua was trying to move Lewis on his own, lifting him up to a sitting position and then trying to pull him to his feet. Starla heard Lewis's groans of pain and felt them as if they were her own. *If only she hadn't called him… If only she hadn't left him at all this last time… She should have stayed in Rabbit Lake with him… and with her daughter.*

Starla dragged herself up from her seat and stepped forward just as Joshua managed to lift Lewis to a semi–standing position. She ducked under Lewis's arm, grabbed him around the waist and tried her best to support him as Joshua stepped out of the vehicle.

Joshua ended up taking most of Lewis's weight, Starla almost falling out of the van on top of them.

Missy didn't bother to close the van door before beginning to back up but called out to Joshua that she'd follow them in after she'd parked.

Joshua continued to be the main support as the three of them staggered unsteadily towards the door.

The security guard intercepted them, shining a light in their eyes and asking, "You guys drunk?"

"Could you give us a hand?" Joshua spoke through gritted teeth. "My friend here is hurt."

"Should've called an ambulance," the man said but obliged as far as pressing the automatic door release.

The emergency waiting room was crowded and there weren't three chairs empty beside each other. Joshua eased Lewis down into a chair and Starla dropped into the one beside him. "I'll go sign him in," Joshua said.

Lewis leaned his head back against the wall. Starla, sighing with relief, did the same.

She felt as if she might pass out at any moment.

"Starla!"

She focused her eyes on Joshua, seeing first his puzzled frown and then the clipboard he thrust into her hands.

"I need your help to fill this out," he said, enunciating each word as he carefully eyed her. "Lewis's birth date and his Health Card number…"

"I—I don't know…" she began.

"You must know his birthday," Joshua replied impatiently. "And you're married. His number will be on your card, same as yours is on his. Just let me see your card."

Starla looked down at her lap. Her bag… She always carried her handbag with her… She must have left it behind when the police had picked her up or more likely, someone had stolen it when she was passed out.

She raised her eyes. "I don't have it."

"My wallet," Lewis rasped. "Back pocket…" He leaned forward a little, groaning as he did.

Joshua quickly reached behind him. "I got it," he said, pulling out Lewis's wallet as he spoke.

He moved to the other side of the room again and Starla leaned back and closed her eyes.

When the call came, it was Missy and Joshua who helped Lewis to his feet. They barely spoke to Starla, all their focus on Lewis.

Starla wondered if she should just leave. Find a dark corner somewhere in the city where no one would find her until it was too late. Or maybe she'd just walk in front of a car—that would be quicker.

What possible difference could it make to anyone?

She tried to summon the energy to stand.

Her eyes drifted shut again.

"Are you coming?"

Missy's sharp voice pierced through the fog.

Starla opened her eyes and Missy's face swam into focus.

She was standing in front of her, hands on hips, looking angry, tired and frazzled.

Starla looked around. The waiting room was much emptier. Joshua and Lewis weren't in any of the chairs.

Starla focused back on Missy. "Lewis…?"

"We've already got him in the van," Missy snapped impatiently. "So, are you coming or what?"

"I—I guess so," Starla said, struggling to her feet.

She started to feel herself falling and then she felt Missy's strong grip on her arm.

"What's the matter with you?" Missy demanded.

But Missy wasn't waiting for an answer and Starla had to focus all her energy on keeping up with Missy's angry strides.

Missy let go of her abruptly as they reached the van and Starla fell forward on her knees in the wet slush.

Missy turned back. "Are you drunk?" she hissed angrily.

Starla barely managed the one word, "No."

"What's wrong?" Joshua called out.

Missy helped her to her feet and opened the van door for her. "You on drugs?"

"No," Starla said, stepping up into the van.

"Are you pregnant?"

Starla met Lewis's eye at that moment. "No."

Missy pulled the door shut behind her and Starla dropped into her seat, thankful when the interior lights were off again and she could sink into the darkness and shut out the world around her.

It seemed as if no time had passed at all before Starla heard the van door being pulled open, and the interior light came on again. She tried to lift her arm to shield her eyes but it felt like a lead weight.

She heard them helping Lewis out. Maybe they would just forget about her... Leave her here...

But Missy was back. "C'mon," she said, "You think we're going to carry you in too?"

Starla struggled to sit up but found she was too weak.

"C'mon," Missy said impatiently, grabbing her by the arm.

And once moving, Starla found she could keep going.

It helped that Missy was half dragging her. But Starla wished that she wouldn't walk so fast...

The door was ajar. Missy pushed it open and led Starla to a chair.

It was an easy chair, comfortable by hotel room standards.

Starla slipped her shoes off, pulled her knees up and rested her head on the arm of the chair. *She was so cold. And so tired!*

Missy immediately turned her attention to Joshua who was helping Lewis. He'd already pulled back the sheets and blankets and taken Lewis's boots off. Missy helped him to ease Lewis down onto the bed and pull the covers over him.

Lewis had his eyes closed again before his head touched the pillow.

"He'll need some more pain medication in a couple of hours," Joshua said, glancing at his watch.

"What—" Starla's hoarse voice cracked but she forced the words out past her dry throat. "What did the doctor say?"

Joshua looked intently at her before replying. "Three cracked ribs and a broken collarbone. There isn't anything they can do. They just said it would take time to heal."

The words, quietly spoken, drove like a knife through her heart. It was her fault and hers alone. She should never have called him.

"There's some pain medication. He'll need another dose in a couple of hours," Missy said.

Starla nodded. She would stay awake. Somehow she would do it.

"You look cold," Joshua said.

Missy rolled her eyes. "Not exactly dressed for the weather," she said in a disgusted tone. "You should at least have a jacket on over that *thing*."

Starla curled in on herself even more, wishing the chair would swallow her whole. She'd had a jacket on when she'd left the day before. She'd had her handbag, too. Now she didn't have either of them. And she had no explanation to offer.

"I'll get you a blanket," Missy said in a gentler tone.

Starla heard the closet door opening and then Missy was back, a hotel issue blanket in hand. She shook it open but hesitated before laying it on top of Starla. "Your pants are wet where you fell," she said.

Starla shook her head. "I don't have anything else to wear."

"Maybe I have something…" Missy began. But Lewis was trying to say something. Joshua, closest to him, understood and repeated it for the others. "He said 'bag.' He has a packsack out in the van. I'll go get it."

"This will help for now," Missy said, tucking the blanket around Starla as Joshua headed out the door.

He was back a moment later loaded down with their overnight bag, Lewis's packsack, some bottles of water and a donut box.

Missy relieved him of two of the bottles of water that were starting to slip out of his arms. She turned towards Starla. "Would you like a drink?"

Starla didn't really feel that thirsty. Just incredibly tired…

But Missy didn't wait for a reply. She unscrewed the cap and handed one to Starla; then opened one for herself as well.

Starla took a sip of the water and then grabbed at the bottle with both hands and began to gulp it down. In her panic, she started to choke and began to cough and sputter.

She was okay again in a moment but embarrassed by her actions. She didn't know what had come over her! Except that before she hadn't even realized she was thirsty and now suddenly she felt as if she could drink a whole lake!

Missy and Joshua were both staring at her.

Starla raised the bottle to her lips again. Joshua walked quickly towards her. "Just take it slow this time," he advised.

Starla managed to control the urge to gulp it all down.

But she was ready for more…

Missy handed her another bottle and Starla drank this one more slowly.

"When did you last have something to drink?" Joshua asked.

Starla shook her head. She couldn't remember. "I've been so tired."

"When did you last eat?"

Starla shook her head again. "It's been a while…"

"Have you just been living on the streets?"

Starla wished he would stop asking so many questions! "No, a house…"

"And they didn't feed you—or give you any water to drink!"

"I—I haven't earned—kitchen privilege in—in quite a while. I got water from the bathroom sometimes—when I felt well enough."

"Kitchen privilege!" Missy exclaimed. "Starla, eating is not a privilege. It's a necessity!"

"They wouldn't give you food?" Joshua asked gently.

Starla lowered her eyes. "I—I wasn't working. You don't get to eat if you don't work." She hazarded a glance at Lewis and saw a flash of anger in his eyes.

Joshua stood suddenly to his feet. "There's donuts…"

Lewis's eyes closed again. Starla bowed her head. Her cheeks felt hot. She wished she could just disappear. She wished that she'd never called them.

"Here," Joshua said, holding the donut box open for her. "It's not the greatest thing to eat on any empty stomach but it's better than nothing."

Missy had opened the packsack. "There's a pair of jeans in here, if you want to change," she said.

Starla shook her head. The plain yeast donut she was eating

tasted like the best thing she'd ever had in her life. But it was taking all her strength just to lift the food to her mouth. She couldn't imagine the effort it would take to get up and change her clothes.

"There's a jacket here, too."

Starla looked and saw her warm red flannel bush jacket. "Please…"

The jacket was warm and reminded Starla of all the good things that she'd once had. Walking in the bush with Lewis and Karissa… Sitting around a fire…

"Are you going to be okay now?" Missy asked. "I think I need to head to bed myself pretty soon."

"Yes, I'll be fine. Thanks."

"It's okay," Missy said, patting her arm before stepping away.

Joshua had moved a desk chair over to sit beside the bed. "I'll come and join you in a minute, honey," he said.

Lewis's eyes were still closed. Starla hoped that the pain medication was working and that he was able to sleep.

Joshua watched him in silence for a few moments before shifting slightly in his seat to face Starla. "We should have called the police," he said.

"No!" she gasped.

Joshua turned fully to face her. "Why not?" he demanded. "Lewis has three cracked ribs and a broken collarbone!"

Starla winced and looked away. "I've never seen him so angry," she whispered. "I've never seen him do anything like that before."

"Who are you talking about?" Joshua asked. "The same person who kept you locked up in some *house* until you were half starved to death?"

"I—I was there by my own choice," Starla protested weakly.

Joshua shook his head and turned away, his focus again on

Lewis, who had remained silent throughout, his eyes still closed.

"I'm glad you called us," Joshua said in a weary voice.

"I should have waited at the police station."

Joshua swiveled around again. "Yes," he said emphatically, "you should have! Why didn't you?"

"I—I don't know," Starla answered truthfully. "The police officers were looking at me strange. They expected you to be there sooner. I told them it was a long ways away. I said you'd be there... Then... I don't know. It was as if the walls were closing in around me. I needed to get some fresh air. I was walking around outside a bit and then I thought I saw Denny and Rick. I knew I had to get out of there..."

"Denny and Rick?" Joshua prompted.

"They—they were the ones who—who held Lewis."

Joshua leaned towards her. "I didn't see what happened, Starla. Denny and Rick were the ones who beat up Lewis?"

Starla turned away from his intense gaze. "No," she said, "it wasn't them. They just held him. I—I've never seen Eric so angry. It was like he hated Lewis. I don't know why."

"Think I could make a guess."

Starla was surprised by the sarcasm thick in Joshua's voice. She turned towards him again as he continued, "So, let's get back to why you didn't wait for us at the police station. You were afraid of these two... Denny and Rick."

"Not really afraid," Starla corrected. "Well, maybe I was a bit afraid, especially of Denny. And I thought they might talk me into going back. I decided to just walk around town for a while and then come back later."

Starla paused. Things were a bit fuzzy in her memory after that. "I—I guess I ended up getting disoriented somehow. I couldn't find my way back to the station. And I was just so tired… I had to sit down. I guess I fell asleep or—or something."

"When I saw you, you seemed to be alone," Joshua began in a slow thoughtful voice. "How did they know you were there? How did they know we were coming?"

Starla shook her head. She'd heard Lewis's voice and then suddenly Denny and Rick were there—and Eric. Tears sprang to her eyes. "He knows everything. He always knows what we're doing, where we're going…"

She saw the doubt in Joshua's eyes. How could she possibly explain what her life was like? Eric kept tabs on everything they did or said. He told them it was for their own good.

"Denny and Rick—they help him," she said. "They're always on the street watching out for us. It's like a protection for us. We're safe. And—and Eric knows right away if we're—if we're cheating on him."

Joshua glanced at Lewis before turning incredulous eyes on Starla. "Cheating on *him?*"

Starla averted her eyes. "With—with other—"

"With other *pimps*," Joshua said angrily.

Starla wished he would leave. Why was he still in the room?

When next he spoke, Joshua's voice was surprisingly gentle. "That's no kind of a life, Starla."

She bit her lip to keep the sob of pain from escaping but she could do nothing to hold back the scalding tears that filled her eyes and flowed down her cheeks.

"I'm glad you had the courage to leave," Joshua said.

"*Courage?*" Starla spat out the word. "Courage! I don't have courage. I'm always running. Running home. Running away. Running home again. Running away again. I don't have *courage!* I'm always afraid." Her voice trailed off. "Always…"

Joshua's eyes were filled with compassion. "Starla," he said, "Courage isn't about not being afraid. It's about doing what we know we should do *even when we are afraid*."

Starla shook her head. What could Joshua possibly know about fear? He was a man.

"And fear can be a good thing," Joshua continued, "if it gets us out of a dangerous spot."

Starla just shook her head again. Fear had never gotten her out of anything. It had just driven her from one "dangerous spot" to another.

"Fear is a natural response—something that God built into us," Joshua continued with a gentle smile. "So we don't do stupid things like run in front of a car—or jump off mountains. The thing to think about is—does your fear move you forward or hold you back? Does it make you put your seat belt on—or does it prevent you from driving at all? Does it make you study hard for an exam or does it paralyze you so you can't write the exam at all?"

"It paralyzes me—at least for a while," Starla said thoughtfully. "But most often it makes me want to run. And it seems as if it never really ever goes away either. It's something that's always with me. I'm either a little bit anxious or really afraid—or I'm terrified." Starla smiled nervously up at him. "I guess that makes me sound crazy or something."

"No," Joshua said. "I remember feeling that way myself. And sometimes it still creeps up on me and I find myself feeling anxious—or afraid—or even terrified. And I have to tell you, there aren't any really, easy simple answers."

Starla smiled, relieved that he hadn't tried to give her one of those "easy simple answers." She'd heard enough of those in her lifetime!

"What really helped me," Joshua continued, "was finding out that there were people in the world that I could trust. And then knowing that I could also trust God."

"Not the other way around?" Starla asked doubtfully.

"No." Joshua shook his head. "Maybe it should be. Or maybe it's just the way that God designed things. That's why he gave us parents, I think, so we can learn about trust. But if we have parents who don't take care of us properly or worse yet, abuse their children, then somehow later in life, that child will need to learn trust from another person."

"I've always been told that I should just trust in God and not be afraid."

"Yeah, I know." Joshua sighed. "But like I said, sometimes if trust has been broken and the people who should have cared for and protected a child, don't, then it can sometimes be just too big of a leap to trust God who we cannot see or feel."

Starla nodded. And turned away. It was too much to take in all at once. She needed time to think about it. And she *was* very tired. She laid her head down on the arm of the chair again.

Joshua stood to his feet. "You should really have something more nutritious than donuts and water. Maybe I can find a vending machine and at least get you some juice or something."

He paused in the doorway. "You'll be okay?"

Starla nodded and Joshua left.

She looked over at Lewis. He was lying so still.

"Lewis…" she whispered into the silence.

He didn't respond. He hadn't spoken to her at all since he'd found her. Starla knew it was because he was so badly injured.

But she longed for him to say something to her—anything.

"Lewis..." she said a little louder.

But still he didn't answer her.

Starla laid her head down again and felt her hand become wet with tears.

HE'D HEARD HER BUT FELT incapable of a response. It was just too much of an effort physically and emotionally.

And he had no idea how he was going to make it through the next few days and weeks and months.

She was his wife. She was back.

But she had shared her heart more with Joshua in the last ten minutes than she had with Lewis in the past twenty-two months that they'd been married.

And he had no idea how to change that. Or even if he wanted to try anymore.

Kitchen privileges...

What kind of a man would starve the very people who were working for him? And what kind of place was this 'house'?

He didn't want to know.

He didn't want to know any of it. He never had.

People would tell him things sometimes—about seeing Starla in Winnipeg with some guy. But he'd closed his ears—and his heart. He told himself he was being loyal to her—not wanting to believe the rumors.

But he'd just been too afraid.

She'd never said anything before about where she stayed in Winnipeg or what it was like. He'd never asked.

Now he'd probably met the man she'd lived with there—she and the others. Starla was just one of his "girls"—one of his "best girls." He didn't want to know what that meant. He especially didn't want to know what "privileges" went with the title of being "Number One."

Lewis was grateful when he heard the room door open. He didn't want to be alone with his thoughts anymore. Even if he had to listen to Starla and Joshua have another heart–to–heart conversation…

But she seemed to have fallen asleep. At least she didn't respond when Joshua spoke her name.

"Are you awake, Lewis?"

It was all he could do just to open his eyes. It seemed way too much of an effort to speak.

"I should probably get some sleep," Joshua said. "If we're going to head back tomorrow… It really depends on how you feel. We could stay another night but it would be nice to be home for Easter Sunday…"

What did it matter? What possible difference could it make?

"I guess you won't be in any shape to play drums…"

"Yeah," Lewis managed to speak in a hoarse whisper. He was trying hard not to move. It hurt to breath—it hurt more to talk.

"How do you feel?" Joshua persisted.

"Lousy."

"Do you want me to stay here with you? Starla seems to be asleep. You might need help later in the night…"

Lewis closed his eyes. *He wanted him to stay. He wanted him to go.*

"Maybe I could set my alarm for a couple of hours from now and come in and check on you then," Joshua suggested.

"Okay," Lewis mumbled.

"Is there anything you need right now?"

"No."

"There's some water and your bottle of pain pills on the bedside table here," Joshua said. "And I'll leave the bathroom light on."

Lewis was relieved when he finally heard the hotel room door open and then close again. Unless the pain got a whole lot less, he probably wouldn't sleep at all. But at least he wouldn't have to talk either.

STARLA WOKE UP A LITTLE STIFF from sleeping curled up in a chair. But she felt surprisingly better than she had the day before. Just very, very thirsty still—and a little bit hungry, too.

The bathroom light had been left on and there was the faintest crack of daylight coming through between the curtains.

Lewis appeared to be asleep. Starla walked quietly over to the bed and looked down. He seemed a little more relaxed than he'd been the night before. He was rolled over on his side facing the outside door—and the night table. The bottle of pills had been knocked over. A few tablets were on the table and a couple had fallen on the floor. There was an empty glass of water.

Starla hoped that Lewis hadn't taken too many of the pills. But he looked okay and his breathing seemed to be deep and even.

She walked towards the bathroom. The empty glass had reminded her again of how thirsty she was.

She drank two glasses of water and then thought maybe she should wait a while before drinking more. And she did feel hungry, too.

The box of donuts was still on top of the desk where Joshua had left them. There was also a can of orange juice and a package of crackers with peanut butter. Starla ate the crackers and drank the juice. Then she had a donut with chocolate icing and one with lemon filling.

It felt good to have food in her stomach again. And someone must have turned the heat up in the room. She wasn't feeling so shivery cold anymore. The jacket probably helped, too. It was so warm and it evoked so many warm memories. It had been kind of Lewis to bring it for her.

But that was who he was—kind and good.

And Missy had said something about a pair of pants that were in the bag, too. Starla found the packsack over by the coat rack and eagerly opened it. She couldn't help smiling when she saw the green mints that she liked so well. Lewis had thought of everything. And he'd packed her a full set of clothes and even a dry pair of shoes. And there was shampoo and conditioner and a brush and some bits of makeup that she'd left at home. She'd had some in her handbag. But that was gone now.

Starla tried to mentally check off what had been in her bag—things she would now have to replace. Her Indian status card, her OHIP health card, some makeup, a pair of earrings…

Suddenly she groaned and shook her head in frustration. She'd lost it—for the second time! Starla leaned up against the wall and looked at Lewis wondering if he'd forgive her as easily as he had the first time she'd lost the wedding band he'd given her.

They of course weren't allowed to wear anything like that when they were working and it was just easier to keep it safe in a zippered pocket in her handbag. But now it was lost—almost certainly gone for good.

Lewis sure wouldn't want to give her a third wedding band after she'd lost the first two!

Starla wasn't as excited about what was in the packsack now. She felt bad that Lewis had gone to such an effort and she'd lost the one thing that would mean the most to him.

But it did feel good to be in her own clothes again and to have a shower and wash her hair.

At least she felt clean on the outside. There'd only been once or twice in her whole life when she'd felt clean on the inside. And that feeling hadn't lasted long. Only as long as it took for the memories to come crashing in again. Crushing the life out of her…

Starla quietly moved the desk chair away from beside the bed and pulled the big chair that she'd been sleeping in over instead.

She sat down with her elbows on the arms of the chair and her chin resting in her folded hands. She was still so tired.

But mostly she felt sad.

Lewis opened his eyes at that moment and Starla felt sadder still. He looked so beat up, physically and emotionally.

She longed to put her arms around him. But didn't know if she had the right to do that anymore.

And would he accept comfort from her? He'd always been the stronger one of the two of them—the one who usually supported her.

He still hadn't spoken a word and Starla desperately needed to hear his voice. But she didn't know what to say or how to begin.

She hoped that Lewis would sense her hesitation and her anxiety and be the first one to start the conversation.

But he interpreted her silence in a much different way.

His voice was hoarse with pain or suppressed emotions but his words fell with the blow of a sledgehammer.

"Still trying to decide which one of us you want?"

Chapter 5

STARLA REELED FROM THE IMPACT of his words.

"No!" she gasped. "There's—there's nothing to decide. You're my husband."

He looked away from her. "Am I?"

Starla grabbed the arms of her chair. *What was he trying to tell her? Had he decided to divorce her? But why had he come for her then?*

"Aren't you?" she asked weakly.

But her question went unanswered and Starla's panic grew as the minutes passed.

"Lewis..." she finally spoke into the silence.

He turned back towards her and the look in his eyes told her more than anything he could possibly have said.

In that moment, Starla had a glimpse of the deep pain that she had caused and in that moment, felt deep remorse.

"I'm sorry," she whispered.

But if anything her words seemed to increase the pain rather than diminish it. He shut his eyes again and Starla was shocked to see a tear roll down his cheek followed by another and then another.

She couldn't ever remember him crying.

And no sound came from his lips now—no heaving sobs—just

that silent steady flow of tears.

Starla had no idea what to do. He'd always been the one to comfort and help her. He'd been the one to get up in the night with Karissa. He'd been the one who most often fed her daughter and bathed her and dressed her in the morning so that Starla could have time to get herself ready before they left for the camp. And he'd often helped with the cooking and cleaning, too. And he was always doing little things to please her. Like buying the green mints that she liked…

But now he was hurting and she had no idea how to help him. Or if he would even accept any help from her.

She was the one causing his pain.

A perfunctory knock was followed immediately by a cheery "good morning" from Joshua.

Then he saw their faces and his whole demeanor changed.

He walked quietly over to them, glanced down at Lewis and then back up at Starla. "You guys need more time?" he asked gently.

Lewis answered in a strained voice, "No." And Starla shook her head sadly. She had to agree with Lewis. What good would more time do?

"I'm sorry I forgot to set my alarm. I meant to come in and check on you in the night," Joshua continued. "How are you feeling?" he asked Lewis and then glanced up at Starla including her in the question.

But their faces told him all he needed to know and it seemed that neither of them could find the strength to put what they were feeling into words.

"We were thinking about heading out soon," Joshua said. "Do you feel well enough to travel, Lewis?"

Joshua waited for his brief nod of approval before continuing,

"Maybe I could help you up to the bathroom first."

Lewis nodded again and Joshua helped him to stand up. It was difficult because every bit of movement seemed to cause Lewis pain. Starla wasn't sure he was going to be able to walk even the short distance to the bathroom. He seemed very unsteady on his feet.

She stood up quickly to go on the opposite side from Joshua.

But as she touched Lewis's arm, she felt him instantly recoil. She stepped back quickly and let them pass, Lewis leaning heavily on Joshua as they made their way slowly across the room.

Starla curled back up into the chair she'd vacated, pulling her bush shirt close around her. She felt cold again.

I've lost my best friend, she thought. *My very best friend.*

JOSHUA KNEW IT HAD NOT gone well between the two of them. They both had that look of bleak despair when all is lost. He'd seen pictures of war victims who looked like that—their homes destroyed, their families divided, all that they had cherished lost forever.

And he knew there was little he could do.

They had prayed—a lot. He and Missy and others had been praying for Starla and Lewis ever since she'd left this last time.

In many ways, God was their only hope—the only One who could heal the gaping wounds that were so evident—wounds that could well be fatal if not tended to by the Great Healer.

Joshua went to the front desk to check them out of the hotel. No one had wanted breakfast. Missy was having a bout of morning sickness again and Lewis and Starla both just shook their heads when Joshua asked if they were hungry. Joshua filled up his travel mug with a complimentary coffee from the hotel and grabbed one of the donuts left in the box. He thought maybe they could stop and get something for lunch later—even if it was just sandwiches from a gas station along the way.

They packed up what little things they had. Starla didn't want to take any of her discarded clothes that had been left in the bathroom—or even her wet shoes that Missy had helped her take off the night before.

"They're not mine," she said, not explaining further.

After everyone was in the van, Joshua prayed out loud for each of them and for the miles that they still needed to cover.

None of them really looked as if they were up to it. Lewis was lying down on the back seat and Starla in the middle. And it wasn't too far into the trip before Missy fell asleep in the front seat beside him.

Joshua didn't mind; he had a lot to think about.

He'd known Starla all her life. Even though she was only six years younger than him, she was his step–brother's daughter so technically he was her uncle, though he'd rarely thought of himself in that way. His father had died when Joshua was fourteen and since that time, Tom Peters had taken on the role of mentor and friend, becoming more of a father than his own father had ever been. Joshua had spent most of his time at Goldrock Lodge and rarely saw any of his biological family.

For many years, he and Tom had talked of having a youth program and when Tom had died suddenly less than a year ago, Joshua had been determined to fulfill their dream. Starla had entered their program in January and for two and a half months, she had been an eager participant, taking courses on the Internet and attending the various classes they had at the camp, always keenly interested in what was being taught. She'd seemed eager to learn how to be a good mom, too. It was hard to understand how she could leave her daughter—and her husband.

People in the community were most sympathetic towards Lewis. It was obvious to everyone that he was making a tremendous effort to be a good husband and a good father.

Joshua wondered sometimes if he was even trying too hard. Maybe it was keeping Starla from growing and developing as she should.

Something was sure wrong somewhere!

He couldn't imagine Missy leaving him. And he couldn't even begin to imagine what would have to happen in their relationship for her to leave him and live with another man—or men.

And how Starla could prefer that over a loving husband, he had no idea!

JOSHUA DECIDED TO LET EVERYONE sleep for as long as possible so they didn't stop again until it was almost 1:00 P.M. and they were in Vermillion Bay, the last service station before Ear Falls.

Joshua bought sandwiches and drinks, and everyone ate at least a little. And though he moved stiffly, Lewis was able to walk the few steps into the service station bathroom and back unaided.

Missy was starting to look a little better, too. She chatted with Joshua for the rest of the drive, which helped to pass the time for both of them.

The flight to Rabbit Lake ended up being much smoother than the way down and Missy didn't look nearly as ill when they landed as she had after their flight the day before.

As they disembarked from the plane and walked towards the terminal, most of the other passengers went on ahead of them. Lewis was still walking slowly, Missy by his side, but Starla was the one who was really holding back. Joshua kept pace with her, wondering if Starla was wishing she was back on the plane again.

Keegan and Randi must have come to the airport to meet them; Joshua smiled as he heard Karissa's joyous cry of "Daddy!"

But suddenly, beside him, he heard a gasp and a faint echo of the same word. "Daddy…"

He was barely in time to catch Starla as she fell.

A crowd gathered quickly around them, asking questions and offering advice as Starla slowly opened her eyes and finally focused them on Joshua.

Someone put a wet paper towel on her forehead. Someone else said that they'd called the Health Center and a nurse was on her way over.

Missy and Joshua helped Starla to her feet and onto a nearby chair.

Starla looked around, her eyes filled with desperation. "Karissa…" she moaned.

"She's right here," Missy said, pointing to a row of chairs opposite them where Lewis sat with Karissa in his lap, Randi seated beside him with Chance in her lap.

But the moment that Starla saw Karissa, she gasped out an anguished "Nooo!" slid to her knees and began to cry hysterically.

Joshua stared in disbelief as she rocked back and forth crying, "No, no, no!"

Missy knelt down and put a comforting arm around her, speaking in a soothing voice, trying her best to calm Starla down.

Joshua looked up at Lewis and Karissa, wondering what could possibly have disturbed Starla so much. Karissa had a cute little blue hair band that matched her fancy blue dress. She had her white winter boots on and her regular winter coat on, unzipped and open since they were inside a building.

Lewis was staring at his wife in shocked silence but Karissa had begun to cry as soon as her mother had. And she was struggling in Lewis's arms. She pushed suddenly with her hands and knees against Lewis's chest and he flinched in pain and looked down at his daughter in bewilderment.

"Lewis…" Joshua stepped forward. "I can take her if you'd like."

Lewis lifted his eyes, looking suddenly like a moose stunned by the headlights of a car.

Then as Joshua lifted Karissa from his arms, Lewis's face melted into a look of abject grief. He cried out "You can take them both!" and turned and stumbled towards the door.

Joshua didn't want to run after him while holding Karissa and was relieved when Keegan stepped forward. "I'll go," he said, hurrying after his brother.

Joshua had no time to think about what he should have done differently. The nurse had arrived and was asking for his help to lift Starla up onto the seat again. Missy took Karissa out of his arms and moved a few steps away from them cooing softly to the little girl and patting her on the back as she walked.

"We should get her over to the Health Center," the nurse said. "She'll likely need a sedative but we need to know a little more about her—"

"No!" Starla cried. "Let me stay with my baby—please—please let me stay with my baby!"

"Starla," Joshua said firmly, "you're going to have to calm down a little if you want to be with Karissa."

She stared wildly at him, realizing suddenly that he no longer had her daughter. She stood to her feet, blind terror on her face until her eyes fastened on Missy holding Karissa, just a few feet away from them.

Starla made a visible effort then to control her runaway emotions. But as she sank back down onto the seat again, she didn't take her eyes off Karissa for even an instant.

"That's it, dear," the nurse said, rubbing Starla's back as she spoke. "Just take some deep breaths. Your daughter's okay. She's in good hands…"

"She hasn't seen her for a month," Joshua offered. But even as he spoke the words, he knew the long absence didn't explain Starla's hysteria. The last time she'd been away from Karissa, she'd been gone for seven months and there hadn't been anything like this kind of reaction when she'd arrived back.

Karissa's crying had subsided into hiccupping sobs and though tears were still coursing down Starla's cheeks, her crying had been reduced to long, shuddering gasps as she tried very hard to not further alarm her daughter.

But when the nurse suggested that they should perhaps go for a brief visit to the Health Center, Starla screamed, "No!" and Karissa began to cry again.

"Maybe if we could just go somewhere quiet," Joshua suggested. There was still a small group of concerned people gathered around them at the airport.

The nurse looked at him skeptically. She was new to the community and had never met Joshua before. "Are you a relative?" she asked.

"Yes, I'm her uncle."

"You seem a little young for that."

Joshua didn't feel the need to explain why there was sixteen years difference in age between he and Starla's father. She had asked if he was a relative and he was.

"We could call you—later—if we need to," Joshua suggested.

The nurse patted Starla's knee. "You going to be okay, now?" she asked, eying her carefully.

Starla nodded, once more making an obvious effort at self-control.

"You'll take her home?" the nurse asked Joshua.

"To our house," Joshua said cautiously, watching closely for Starla's reaction. "Karissa will come with us, too."

She seemed unable to stop the steady flow of tears but Starla managed to nod and even convey some gratitude with a tremulous smile in Joshua's direction.

"We brought the van," Randi said, stepping forward. The nurse eyed her carefully, too. But there was nothing to fault in Randi's calm demeanor or physical appearance. She wore a navy jacket with screen-printing of "Goldrock Lodge" on it and dark blue cargo pants, her shiny black hair worn in a single thick braid over her left shoulder.

She was carrying her nine-month-old son, Chance, the bag that Lewis had packed for Karissa, and the packsack that she must have picked up from baggage already.

Joshua noted that Missy had their overnight bag slung over her shoulder and had Karissa ready to go with her jacket zipped, and her hat and mitts on.

The nurse walked with them out of the terminal. "Call the Health Center if you have any concerns at all," she said.

Joshua promised that he would.

Joshua hesitated only a moment before helping Starla into the front passenger seat; Randi and Missy would get the two children into car seats in the back.

The nurse stood watching them until they pulled away.

Starla was still crying silent tears when they got to the camp and Joshua helped her down out of the van and into the lodge, Randi and Missy close behind them with Chance and Karissa and their small amount of luggage.

Good smells greeted them as they opened the door and Randi said that she'd made a pot of moose soup for everyone. She'd serve it up when they were ready.

Missy sat down with Karissa on a chair close to the door and started to take the little girl's coat off.

And suddenly, Starla was off again—moaning and crying.

Missy stood up with Karissa, dropping her coat on the chair as she gently pressed the little girl's head against her chest and covered her opposite ear with her hand. She walked quickly away from them, ignoring Starla's desperate cries.

Joshua grabbed Starla's arm. "She's just going a little ways away," Joshua assured her. "You don't want Karissa to get all upset again, do you?"

Starla tore her eyes away from her daughter, sank down into a chair and doubled over, groaning as if in deep pain.

She was saying something but Joshua couldn't at first understand the words. Then he listened in disbelief as Starla moaned, "I have to go again. I have to take her with me. We can't stay here. I have to go…"

Chapter 6

JOSHUA GLANCED OVER AT MISSY who had stopped and turned back towards them, the shocked look on her face clearly showing that she had also heard what Starla had said.

Joshua eased down onto a chair beside Starla, his mind racing.

"You just got here," he finally said.

She looked up at him and enunciated each word slowly and with obvious difficulty. "I—have—to—go."

"Why?" Joshua asked desperately. "Why do you have to go?"

But Starla was on her feet now. Her voice still shook but her decision seemed to have stopped the flow of tears, if only temporarily. "Give me my daughter," she said, walking towards Missy.

Joshua moved quickly forward. "Maybe we could all eat something first—before you go."

Starla dropped her arms. "I couldn't eat," she whispered as if the very thought repelled her. "But—but you can feed Karissa if you want to."

As Missy headed towards the kitchen, Starla stood watching her, clutching her coat tightly around her.

"Are you cold?" Joshua asked. "I was going to light a fire."

Starla shivered and nodded. It took a moment but she finally tore her eyes away from the kitchen and made a move towards the south end of the lodge where there was a sitting area and fireplace.

Joshua followed her over, grabbed some pieces of wood that were stacked in a pile along the wall close to the fireplace, and bent down to light the fire. When he stood up again, Starla was huddled into a corner of the sofa, staring blankly at the flickering flames.

"You sure you wouldn't like some soup?" Joshua asked.

Starla shook her head.

Joshua hesitated, wondering if there was something more he should do or say.

He was about to leave to join the others in the kitchen when Starla asked in a strained whisper, "Randi—Randi was the one who took care of her?"

"Yes," Joshua said slowly, "her and Keegan. They—they baby-sit her pretty often. She seems to like being there."

Starla gazed intently at him and said, "Please ask Randi where Karissa's clothes are."

"Her—her clothes?" Joshua asked, confused. "I saw Randi bring in a couple of bags, likely one for Karissa and one for Chance."

"I'd like Karissa's bag, please," Starla said, her voice trembling. "And I'd like to have Karissa as soon as she's finished eating."

He conveyed the message to Randi who was as shocked at he and Missy were at the thought of Starla leaving again so soon—and taking Karissa with her this time!

"Lewis…" Randi said in a sorrowful voice.

Joshua nodded. He couldn't begin to imagine how Lewis would react when she left him this time.

"There won't be any more flights out tonight," Missy said, "and I don't even think they'll fly tomorrow since it's Easter Sunday."

Joshua sighed. "We can be thankful for that at least. We have a bit of time to try to talk her out of it."

They prayed before they ate, Joshua asking a special blessing on both Starla and Lewis—and Keegan.

They hadn't heard from the two men yet and Randi said she would try calling him on his cell phone after they were finished eating.

But before they were done, Keegan called her.

He was at Lewis's house and he told Randi that he thought that maybe he should stay there for a little while yet. Randi offered to bring some soup over for them and Keegan gladly accepted her offer.

After Randi finished her call, she asked, "You don't need me here anymore, do you?"

"No, we should be okay," Joshua said, glancing towards the south end of the lodge where Starla was. "The main thing for you and Keegan to do is keep an eye on Lewis. I'm really worried about him."

Randi smiled. "Keegan's always watched over his little brother."

Joshua nodded and smiled in return. But as Randi took her son out of the high chair and went to pack her things, Joshua continued to reflect on Lewis and Keegan's relationship. It seemed in some ways as if Lewis had always followed his older brother—no matter if it was into drugs and alcohol—or if it was into Christianity. Lewis had even talked about going away for police training. But then he'd married Starla. The two brothers had certainly disagreed about that! Keegan had done everything he could to talk his 17–year–old brother out of marrying a sixteen–year–old girl who was five months pregnant with another man's child. In the end though, Keegan had relented and become Lewis's best man and Randi had stood with Starla as her maid of honor.

"Joshua…" Missy interrupted his thoughts. "Would you mind

giving Randi a ride? Keegan has their truck over at Lewis's."

"Uh, sure." Joshua stood to his feet. He was anxious to see how Lewis was doing anyway.

Joshua ended up dropping off Randi and Chance first, since Chance was getting a bit fussy and Randi wanted to get him to bed.

Joshua brought the soup into Lewis's house. He could see that the bedroom was dark and assumed that Lewis was probably lying down.

Keegan was sitting at the kitchen table with a cup of tea in his hands.

"How's it going?" Joshua greeted him.

But when Keegan looked up, there was anger in his eyes. "What happened to my brother?" he asked in a cold hard voice.

Joshua sank down into a kitchen chair opposite him. "I don't really know," he said quietly.

"He went to Winnipeg with you. He came back with you. And you say you don't know what happened!"

"We were apart for a short time. I was parking the van—"

"Lewis says you didn't even call the police."

"Lewis said that?"

"Yeah—when I asked him."

"I didn't think he wanted me to," Joshua carefully explained. "I know for sure that Starla didn't want them to be called."

Keegan jumped to his feet. "What Starla wants has got nothing to do with it! If she wants to protect her friends—"

"That wasn't it," Joshua protested. "She was afraid they'd come back... hurt Lewis more... or Missy and I."

With a huge sigh of exasperation, Keegan sank back down in his chair. He ran a hand through his hair and sighed again. When he spoke, his voice was quiet and sad. "He's in pretty bad shape."

Keegan lowered his voice still more. "It's like he's just shut down completely. I thought at first it might even be something physical like a head injury. But then he spoke quite clearly to me and said that he'd rather be left alone."

Keegan slowly shook his head. "I can't leave him like this."

Neither of them spoke for a minute then Keegan asked about Randi, and Joshua told him that he'd driven her and Chance home.

Joshua stood up. "I should really get back. I left Missy alone with Starla. She's…" Joshua hesitated. It didn't seem the right time to tell Keegan that Starla was planning to leave again. "She's not doing so well either," he finally said. "I think maybe she'll be staying at the lodge for the night."

Keegan stood up then, too. He sounded more frustrated than angry as he asked again, *"What happened out there?"*

"I don't know," Joshua spoke honestly. "I know bits and pieces but…" He hesitated again. "I don't think it's going to be an easy reconciliation like the last time."

Keegan shook his head. "I could never understand why she wanted to leave him anyway. No one could ask for a better husband."

"Yeah, I know," Joshua said wearily.

"Thanks for bringing the soup."

Joshua nodded, then suddenly remembered…

"Oh, I have some pain medication that they gave him at the hospital," he said, taking the bottle out of his coat pocket and handing it to Keegan. "The last time he had some was just before we got on the plane—so around three o'clock."

Keegan thanked him, glanced at his watch and set the bottle down on the table.

It seemed strangely quiet as Joshua reentered the lodge. But, he had to remind himself, likely part of what he was feeling was just the absence of all the people who had been in t heir program the previous winter. There had been a lot of activities at the lodge throughout the day and often well into the evening.

The table where they'd eaten was cleared off, but as Joshua walked into the kitchen, he could see that the food wasn't put away and the dishes hadn't been done yet. Missy must be with Starla, he thought.

The guestroom door was a little ajar. Joshua knocked, heard Missy call, "yes" and opened the door a little wider.

"May I come in?" he asked.

"Yeah…" But Missy didn't sound quite like herself.

He stepped into the room and saw her standing in the bathroom doorway. She was turned away from him, looking at something or someone in the bathroom.

"Starla's giving Karissa a bath," Missy said without turning to look at him.

Joshua advanced quickly into the room. "Everything all right?"

"No…" Missy glanced up at him. "I don't know…"

"Missy!"

She turned fully towards him then, shutting the bathroom door quietly behind her.

Joshua's eyes widened in concern as he stared at the bathroom.

"She'll be okay for a minute," Missy said. "I've been watching her. Karissa's just playing with some toys now."

But Missy looked wrung out emotionally. Joshua took both of her hands in his. "Missy, what happened?" he asked.

Tears sprang to her eyes. "I just don't know what's wrong with Starla. And I don't know how to help her."

Joshua led her to the bed and they sat side by side on the edge of it. "Something else happened?" he asked gently.

"This…" Missy said, pointing to the floor beside them. "This happened."

Joshua looked down at the dress that Karissa had been wearing. It had been a beautiful satin dress with lace and ruffles and ribbons. Now, it lay crumpled in a heap on the floor. And it looked as if someone had been trying to tear it to shreds!

"What happened?" Joshua asked gently.

Missy stood up suddenly. "Maybe I'll just go check again…"

Joshua couldn't disagree with her.

He heard her talking to Starla and then to Karissa. There were some small splashing sounds and Karissa's baby chatter.

"They're okay," Missy said, shutting the bathroom door behind her a moment later.

She seemed a bit more relaxed as she sat down beside him again. "It was—it was just kind of weird—I didn't know what to do."

Joshua didn't like the sounds of what he'd heard so far. "Tell me everything—from the beginning," he insisted.

"Okay," Missy began with a sigh. "Starla said that she wanted to bath Karissa—and change her clothes."

"Okay…"

"But then she didn't seem to be able to undress her. She kept crying—and not just crying but—but—like before, you know."

Joshua nodded as Missy continued. "Karissa was getting really upset again and I thought about just taking her away—back to the kitchen."

"Uh—huh." Joshua thought that would have been a good idea.

"Suddenly, Starla started tearing at Karissa's dress. There's a whole bunch of tiny little buttons at the back—she couldn't get them undone because she was too upset and she just started to rip and pull at them…"

Joshua's mind was racing. They shouldn't have let Starla have Karissa for even a minute! Maybe they should have brought her to the hospital. A sedative would have helped at least temporarily. It was wrong for Karissa to be drawn into this.

"I didn't want to start a tug-of-war with Starla over her daughter," Missy continued, "but she wasn't letting me take her. I started to pray—just a simple, 'Help me, Jesus!' and then suddenly, I just knew. It wasn't about Starla—or Karissa—or me. It was about the dress. I started to help Starla take it off her and the Lord just gave me this tremendous sense of peace. And I was able to calm them both down and get the dress off. I finally got the buttons undone enough to slip Karissa up and out of it. I took her on my lap and held her."

"And Starla…?" Joshua asked cautiously.

Missy's eyes were clouded with concern. "She tried to tear the dress to pieces. But it's pretty strong fabric…"

Joshua looked down at the dress again. Starla had certainly managed to ruin it though.

"I kind of left her to it," Missy continued hesitantly. "I was more concerned about Karissa by that point. I was thinking that a bath might still be a good idea. And I could get her pajamas on and get her settled into bed…"

They both looked towards the bathroom then.

"So I did that," Missy continued. "And Starla finally seemed to calm down after a while. She came into the bathroom and just put her head down on the side of the tub and watched Karissa. I think she's okay now, though," Missy said hesitantly. "She's just seems really, really sad."

The bathroom door opened and Joshua, with one swift movement, kicked the dress underneath the bed.

Starla had Karissa wrapped in a towel. They both seemed calm and relaxed.

Joshua and Missy stood up. Missy put a hand out to touch Starla's arm. "How're you doing?" she asked gently.

But Starla walked past her without speaking and began to get Karissa dressed. She'd chosen a pair of pants and a t–shirt that was as far removed from the frilly dress as was possible. She completed the outfit with a little pair of striped sweat socks and some track shoes.

Starla set the little girl on her feet and Karissa immediately began to toddle towards the door. Starla looked over at Missy and Joshua. "Could you guys watch her for me for just a minute?"

They both readily agreed and together began to follow Karissa out into the kitchen.

A moment later, Starla walked by them with a small bundle of blue cloth in her hands.

Missy picked up Karissa as she and Joshua followed Starla out of the kitchen and into the large dining area.

Starla walked to the end of the room and threw the bundle of cloth into the fire.

Joshua and Missy exchanged a quick glance. "Stay here with Karissa," he told her as he hurried across the room.

He was beginning to put some pieces together in his mind.

Starla had been watching the fire consuming the dress but as she heard Joshua approach, she turned defiantly towards him.

It was too late to snatch it out—even if he thought he could or should do it.

Joshua sank down into an easy chair, letting her know that he was no threat. That he wouldn't try to stop what she was doing, or rather, *had* done.

Chapter 7

STARLA TURNED SLIGHTLY SO THAT she could see the fire and also see Joshua. He didn't seem to be going anywhere, though.

She was relieved that he hadn't tried to stop her. But maybe he hadn't known until too late what she had been planning to do.

There were only small scraps of fabric left. Most of it was ashes.

Joshua wasn't even looking towards the fire. He wasn't looking at her either. He had his head bowed and his eyes closed.

Slowly, Starla began to relax. It was done.

She still had to leave.

And at least now she knew why she'd had to come back.

To get her daughter out.

But she'd picked the worst possible time of the year. The ice road over the lake was gone but no one could travel by boat yet. The only way out was by plane and it was unlikely that there'd be any flights out on Easter Sunday.

Starla moved away from the fire and sank down onto the couch, feeling suddenly completely exhausted once more.

Missy came over with Karissa in her arms and quietly asked Starla if it would be okay to put the little girl to bed.

She did look sleepy with her head resting on Missy's shoulder.

Starla nodded and even tried to return the smile that Missy gave her.

She was grateful to Missy and Joshua. They were being kind to her.

But in the end, even their kindness wouldn't be enough.

"Starla…"

She turned her head slowly towards Joshua. *What was the point of talking? It wouldn't change anything.*

He waited till their eyes met. Then he asked her in a gentle voice, "Whose dress was that?"

Starla felt as if she'd been kicked in the stomach! She doubled over, feeling physical pain as she struggled to rein in her emotions.

How could he know?

How could he know!

"Mine," she whispered, not looking at him.

There was a long silence.

When Joshua finally did speak again, his voice was heavy with sadness. "There's not too much difference in age between us," he said.

Six years…

"I guess for the most part, I was a kid when you were a kid," he continued.

Starla nodded, still not looking up at him.

"Sometimes… Sometimes, you can feel like you're the only one."

Starla felt a rising tide of panic. *What was he trying to tell her?*

"Do you remember—I was thirteen—I guess you would have been about seven—your father went to jail."

Starla felt a surge of anger. "Of course I remember. My mother took off the same day. I never saw her again. I had to go live with my Gookum."

Her Gookum… Her grandmother… Actually her great–aunt—Joshua's Aunt Yvonne… Joshua was silent for a moment, absorbing her words. "I wish I could go back and change that for you. I wish there had been some way that I could have helped you at the time."

"And he wasn't in jail very long," Starla continued angrily. "Then he came back with another woman. She stuck around just long enough to give Grandma another baby to take care of. Then he left, too."

"He had to leave," Joshua said quietly. "There was a band council resolution against him."

"I wish they could have kept him away forever."

Joshua shook his head and smiled sadly. "Band councils change."

Starla gazed into the fire. "My father never changed."

"No."

Starla glanced quickly over at Joshua. Something about the way he'd said that one word…

But he wasn't looking in her direction now. "My father never changed either."

His father… Her grandfather…

Starla felt anger rising up in her again. "So what are you trying to say? That I should excuse my father because *he* had an abusive father? You think that gives him a right to do the things he did?"

Joshua didn't react defensively to her anger. He just seemed very sad. "What I'm trying to say is that there were others…" Missy had returned and taken a seat on the arm of Joshua's chair. As he spoke, she gently rubbed his back. There were tears in his eyes now as he continued, "What I'm trying to say to you is that you're not alone."

Starla felt a tumult of emotions churning within her. But the overriding one was still anger. "And that's supposed to make me feel better?" she demanded. "Knowing that others have suffered too. That doesn't make me feel better—that makes me feel worse!"

"Starla…" Joshua said in the same sad, heavy voice. "What Garby did to you, he did to me also."

Rage and grief collided within her and she almost shouted the words. "He dressed you up in frilly little dresses and—" She couldn't continue.

Joshua shook his head. "No, he tied me to a bunk bed—on a filthy mattress—in a broken–down cabin in the bush."

It was one thing talking about theoretical "other people." It was another thing altogether to be confronted with the awful pain that still echoed in Joshua's voice as he spoke about what had happened to him as a child.

Something that had been frozen for a long time began slowly to melt in Starla's heart.

Tears ran down her cheeks. She swiped at them with her hand. But more came—and then still more.

She felt Missy press a box of Kleenex into her hand. Then she was gently rubbing her back as she had Joshua's.

Starla grabbed a handful of Kleenex and wiped at her eyes and blew her nose. But the tears kept coming as if there was no end.

Joshua leaned towards her. "Sometimes, if we can just tell another person… Share our story with someone else… It's like then we're not carrying the burden alone any more."

Starla nodded. She could feel the truth of what he was saying. But she had no idea where to begin.

Missy spoke for the first time. Her voice was kind. "Starla, have you ever told anyone else about what happened to you?"

Starla tried to sound strong but when she spoke, the word "No" came out as a weak, little child's cry. She gulped back the tears, fighting to hang onto her self-control.

"You're in a safe place," Joshua said gently. "You can stop running now."

Starla shook her head. "But what will you do after I tell you?" she asked, her voice still thick with tears. "Will you tell the police or a social worker or something?"

Joshua hesitated. "If you were under age sixteen," he spoke slowly and carefully, "then I'd have to report what you told me to someone in authority. You understand, Starla, that child sexual abuse is not just a very bad, hurtful thing. It's also against the law."

Starla nodded. *But where did that leave her?*

She followed Joshua's gaze as he looked at the fire. The bundle of clothes had been completely reduced to ashes. As he turned back towards her, Joshua spoke even more carefully than before. "If you think that something may have happened to Karissa... We need to talk about it. And maybe the police will have to be called..."

The panic she felt must have shown on her face for Joshua quickly amended. "Maybe we won't have to. Let's just talk about it first, okay?"

Starla nodded but she was trembling—inside and out.

"Okay, then let's start with this dress..."

No!

"We know this is hard for you," Missy said in a soothing voice. "But for Karissa's sake..."

Starla nodded again. She knew that what they were doing was right. *But it was just so hard!*

Joshua looked tired—and older than his years. "We may have destroyed the only physical evidence that exists but we need to look at some of the circumstantial evidence. Karissa should have been with Randi and Keegan the whole time we were gone. I can't imagine them leaving Karissa with your father, even for a short time—"

"He had her!" Starla struggled to control the rising feelings of panic again. "He had her at the airport."

Joshua sounded surprised. "He did?"

But Missy had seen him, too. "He was holding Karissa when we walked into the terminal. Then, after Lewis was sitting down, Keegan took Karissa and set her down on Lewis's lap."

"That's why you fainted! It explains…" He nodded thoughtfully. "It explains a lot."

He picked up the cordless phone from off the end table between the couch and chair and began to dial a number.

Starla, listening, wished she could hear more than just one half of the conversation:

"Hi, Randi…

"Yeah, we're just talking to Starla and we're trying to figure something out. It's about Karissa…

"What we need to know is if you or Keegan ever left her anywhere—for even a few minutes.

"Nothing's wrong—well, hopefully not. It's just that Starla saw Karissa with her father at the airport.

"Uh–huh.

"Yeah, okay.

"All right.

"Yeah, okay, I'll tell her that.

"Okay, I'll double check with him. Yeah, I don't think so either.

"Thanks, Randi.

"Yeah, you too. Bye."

"What'd she say?" Starla asked breathlessly.

"Good news," Joshua said, smiling broadly. "I just want to confirm it with Keegan." He picked up the phone and dialed another number.

Starla had to wait through another interminable conversation but it was sounding good—*too good to be true!*

By the time Joshua put the phone down again, there were tears of relief in everyone's eyes.

"There was never any time while we were gone when either Randi or Keegan or both of them weren't with her," Joshua confirmed.

"But the dress...?" Starla asked weakly. "And—and I saw him."

"He came over to the lodge a little while before the plane arrived," Joshua explained. "He said he just wanted to give his granddaughter an Easter gift. But Starla, they didn't ever leave her alone with him, not for one minute."

Starla listened carefully as he continued. "Randi didn't know anything about the dress—about what it meant to you. She took Karissa upstairs to change because there's a little potty up in the nursery and she wanted her to use it before they left for the airport. Your father stayed down here. He drove a separate vehicle to the airport—Randi and Keegan took Karissa. Your father just happened to be holding her when we walked through the terminal."

No, he hadn't just happened to be holding her—he'd done it on purpose!

Joshua leaned towards her. "Randi and Keegan had no idea, Starla. They still don't. This kind of thing could happen again—"

Starla jumped to her feet. "No! It won't happen ever again because I'm leaving. I'm taking Karissa with me and I'm never coming back!"

Joshua looked up at her with compassion in his eyes. "I can understand why you would feel that way."

Starla sank back onto the couch. "I wish I could leave tonight."

Neither Missy nor Joshua said anything for a minute. Then Missy began hesitantly, "Starla, can we talk about you again?"

She shook her head. "I don't care about me anymore. I'll—I'll figure something out." Tears sprang to her eyes. "But I won't let the same thing happen to my baby. I'll get her away from here if it's the last thing I do!"

She waited for Joshua to argue with her—to try to change her mind. But his thoughts seemed to be running on a slightly different track. "Are there more of these dresses still around, do you think?"

Starla felt like a balloon with all the air let out of it. "Yes," she whispered.

She could feel Missy draw back, clearly shocked. "How many?" she gasped. "Where? How do you know?"

Starla looked at the fire. It was starting to die down. She wished suddenly that she could put all the dresses in there—every single one of them.

But she'd have to confront her father or her grandma—or both of them.

She trembled just thinking about it.

"Cold?" Joshua asked.

Starla nodded. Missy quickly stood up, saying that she would go turn the heat up. "And maybe I'll make some tea for all of us, too."

Joshua got up to put some more wood on the fire.

"Is it all gone?" Starla asked as he stirred the embers.

"Yeah," he said softly. "It's all gone."

He put several logs on then went outside to get more wood to replenish the pile that was inside.

The fire was blazing nicely now and Starla could feel the warmth from it already. She tucked her feet up and pulled her bush jacket closer around her.

Missy arrived with a large tray containing tea, sandwiches and even a small plate of homemade chocolate chip cookies.

"You didn't have supper," Missy said with a smile. "I thought maybe we should just take a little break and maybe you could try to eat a little."

Starla didn't think she was hungry but when Missy offered her a sandwich, she ate it and when she later offered her a cookie, Starla ate that, too. It seemed that she had been hungry after all.

Or perhaps, for the first time in many hours, she was finally beginning to relax. Her daughter hadn't been harmed as she had suspected.

Missy poured everyone another cup of tea and sat down again on the couch beside Starla. No one spoke for a minute and Starla found herself growing nervous again.

Joshua leaned forward and set down his teacup, and Starla braced herself for the question she knew he would ask.

"Do you know where the dresses are?"

Starla shivered, cold in spite of the fire and her warm, wool jacket.

She didn't try to speak but only nodded this time.

"Are they at your house?" Joshua asked gently.

She shook her head. Tears were rolling down her cheeks again and she didn't trust her voice.

"At Aunt Yvonne's house?"

Starla nodded.

Joshua didn't say anything else for a minute. The fire crackled and a log fell in a shimmer of sparks. Starla took a sip of tea. The warm liquid felt good on her raw throat.

Joshua spoke into the stillness. "But technically, they would be yours, wouldn't they? They were gifts from your father?"

More like wages.

But Starla merely nodded again, unwilling and unable to explain.

Joshua caught and held her eye. "Then they're yours," he said firmly. "Yours to do whatever you want with them."

For an instant, it felt as if she'd been thrown a lifeline.

But no...

"They wouldn't let me," she said in a low, hoarse voice.

"They have to, Starla. We'll find a way."

She nodded. But there was no hope in her heart. She had been a prisoner for so long, how could she believe that someone could unlock the door for her? No, it was impossible.

"If we went over there together..." Missy suggested.

"No," Starla and Joshua answered at the same time, defeat in her voice and resignation in his. Starla looked up in surprise. But her Gookum was his aunt and her father was Joshua's brother. He would know them as well or perhaps even better than she did.

"Maybe," Missy began tentatively, "maybe we should all just sleep on it for now. It's been a rough couple of days."

Joshua agreed. "Yeah, that's probably a good idea."

As everyone stood to their feet, Missy asked Starla if she would like to go to church with them the next day.

Starla shook her head. She couldn't imagine being around a lot of people right now. And everyone would be curious about her—and Lewis.

"I don't like the thought of you being alone here," Joshua said as he picked up the tray and the three of them headed towards the kitchen.

"Neither do I," Missy said.

"Maybe if we lock all the doors," Joshua mused as he set the tray down on the kitchen table.

"Will that be enough?" Missy asked.

"Yes." Joshua sighed, pushing a hand through his hair. "That'll probably be enough. My brother's been arrested for a lot of things but break and enter isn't one of them."

"We'll wake you up in the morning before we go," Missy promised. "And we'll leave Karissa with you—unless you'd like us to take her to church."

"No, I'd feel better if she was here with me—if you don't mind."

"No, I understand," Missy answered quickly.

Karissa was asleep when they went to check in on her. Starla found it hard to tear herself away but Missy and Joshua said that they would leave the nursery and their bedroom doors open and would be able to hear the little girl if she woke up in the night.

There were glass patio doors in the guestroom that opened onto a deck. Joshua made sure these were locked and Missy pulled the curtains shut over them, making the room feel even more secure.

It seemed strange to be sleeping in the lodge as a guest. Starla had been there during the day as a program participant but had never before stayed overnight.

But the instant that Missy and Joshua were gone, Starla felt total exhaustion creep over her. And suddenly, it didn't matter where she was. She climbed into bed, pulled up the blankets and was almost instantly fast asleep.

LEWIS DID NOT FARE as well that night. Though lacking the strength and desire to sit up and talk with his brother, he found that he was also incapable of sleeping.

Keegan had talked him into drinking a cup of tea and later a cup of broth from the soup that Randi had made. And he'd given him another dose of pain medication.

He'd wanted Lewis to go to the Health Center to have a local doctor check him out but Lewis had flatly refused. The doctor in Winnipeg had said there was nothing they could do for him. Lewis was just supposed to stay away from strenuous activity and let things heal on their own.

Well, he wasn't planning on shoveling snow or playing drums for a while.

If ever…

More and more it was getting harder for Lewis to envision a future of any kind. When he tried to look forward, everything just blurred together in his mind. The past, the present, the future… all of it just a dark haze.

When he closed his eyes, the images grew clearer but more frightening and his thoughts collided together in confusion.

He couldn't bear to live without her. But he honestly didn't know if he could live with her either. He was glad that she was up at the lodge—at least for now.

He mostly lay on his back, staring up at the ceiling. If he turned to his right, he saw the empty side of the bed where his sometimes wife slept. If he turned to the left, he saw Karissa's empty crib.

He knew that Joshua and Missy would make sure that she was okay. Karissa was pretty used to them and often napped in the nursery at the lodge.

And he couldn't have taken care of her himself anyway. It hurt even to move. He couldn't imagine taking care of a busy, active toddler.

But he missed her. And he missed his wife. He missed what they'd had this past winter—or at least what he thought they'd had.

He had thought that she loved him.

But she'd gone to live with another man—no, other *men!*

His mind collapsed on the thought. It was just too much—*too much!*

And he was trying. Trying so hard to pull it together. To snap out of it. To pull himself up from the quicksand that he was slowly drowning in.

The room grew suddenly darker and Lewis realized that Keegan had turned off the living room and kitchen lights and must be planning to spend the night sleeping on Lewis's couch.

There was still a bit of light, maybe from the bathroom. Lewis could still make out the shapes of some things—like the empty crib.

He wished that he hadn't run away from them in the airport.

And he wondered how much he was to blame for his wife and child being at the lodge instead of home with him.

He'd taken her back before—what was different this time?

Why was he feeling so betrayed? Even though she had come back to him, it felt as if she was even further away from him than when she had been gone. It didn't make any sense.

But there was something different this time.

Was it just him—or was she different too?

Lewis wished that he could talk to his brother but already he could hear the sound of soft snoring coming from the living room.

Suddenly, Lewis felt overwhelmed by a sense of aloneness. He hadn't realized before how comforting it was to know there was someone else out there awake.

Now he felt totally alone—cut adrift from the rest of the universe.

Abandoned...

But no, she'd come back—and with Karissa too!

She must have come quietly into the room while he was sleeping.

Karissa was lying on top of his chest; Starla was cuddled up beside him, her arm draped over Karissa and Lewis, embracing them both.

No!

It'd only been a dream!

His bed was cold and empty and his arms ached with longing for them.

But wait! There they were—standing at the end of his bed!
And his mother was with them.
They all looked so sad.
They were waving goodbye.
They were leaving. Leaving him forever...

Lewis startled awake.

He felt chilled to the bone.

Maybe the fire had gone out.

He had to get up and check it.

Yes, it had gone out. He'd get some wood from the porch. But he was still cold. So cold...

Chapter 8

K<small>EEGAN WOKE UP FEELING COLD</small>, and realized that he hadn't checked the fire before he went to sleep.

I must have been really tired, he thought, as he stumbled out to the porch and got some wood.

There weren't even a few embers left and Keegan had to find some newspaper and matches to get the fire going again.

He checked on his brother who seemed to be asleep. He was huddled up in a ball as if he was cold but the blankets had been thrown aside as if he was planning to get out of bed. Thankfully, Lewis still had on his jeans, t–shirt and socks.

Keegan pulled the covers back up over him and stood looking down at his brother.

He hadn't always been there for him.

He'd tried, but it seemed that at the most crucial times, he'd failed him.

When their father was imprisoned, Keegan wasn't able to help him. He'd been heavy into gas–sniffing and Lewis had followed in his older brother's footsteps.

Then Colin had come alongside and helped Keegan through high school. But as Keegan spent time with Colin and his wife, Sarah, Lewis was left alone at home with their mother who suffered from chronic depression—a legacy of the years of physical and emotional abuse from their father.

And Keegan was away at police academy and Lewis home alone with their mother when they got the news that their father had died in jail. Keegan had expected that their mother would feel relief. But instead, in that instant, something fragile within her had finally shattered—and she had taken her own life.

Keegan had been on his way back to Rabbit Lake for his father's funeral when he received word of his mother's death. And when he got home, Keegan began to fear for his brother's life as well. Lewis was only fifteen at the time and he blamed himself entirely for his mother's death, feeling that he could have somehow prevented it by doing more or being more. Lewis had gone into a deep depression and had even been suicidal for a while.

And he hadn't really even been there for him when Starla had left that first time. Keegan and Randi had done what they could to help Lewis with two–month–old Karissa but they hadn't been able to do too much. Randi had been going through a very difficult pregnancy at the time. She'd had one miscarriage shortly after they'd been married and the doctors were worried that Randi would lose this one, too. But she hadn't. Seven months later, Chance had been born, a healthy eight–pound baby boy.

Lewis had been pretty upset when Starla had left that time but he'd rallied quickly for Karissa's sake. And he'd done an amazing job. A lot of people had doubted his ability to care for such a young child. But Lewis was willing always to take advice and any offers of help. He was a quick learner and soon even the public health nurses and social workers had to agree that, in this case at least, an 18–year–old boy could raise a baby girl on his own. But it hadn't been easy for him. Lewis had seemed to be in a bit of a daze most of the time, physically tired and emotionally worn down by Starla's absence.

But he'd taken her back with apparent ease. That had amazed everyone, too. Lewis had seemed to forgive her so easily—and take her back without any hesitation.

Keegan sensed that somehow, this time, things were different. It was as if Lewis was more upset now that she was home! And he seemed to have fallen into a deep depression—the same kind of depression as when their mother had died. He had shut down in the same way—wanting to be alone—not talking to anyone—keeping the lights off—not eating.

This time, though, Keegan was determined to stick with him—to see his brother through—even if it meant time away from his family or his job.

It was Easter morning and he knew that Randi would be expecting him to go to church with her and with Chance.

Keegan looked at his watch—8:13 A.M. He should give her a call.

He had phoned her the evening before to let her know that he was going to stay overnight at Lewis's house. She had been okay with that.

But she wasn't too pleased when he called to tell her that he might end up spending the day as well. They had bought an Easter gift for Chance…

Keegan said that he would do his best to get home before church started but he told her that he wouldn't leave his brother if he felt that he needed to stay.

Randi asked him about breakfast but Keegan had already put on a pot of coffee and there was lots of food in the house. He told her they'd be fine.

When he went in to check on Lewis again, his brother was awake, staring over at the crib with a bleak look on his face.

"Did I wake you up?" Keegan asked. "I was just talking to Randi."

Lewis shook his head slightly.

"You want to talk?" Keegan asked, crouching down beside him.

Lewis shook his head again and closed his eyes.

Keegan sighed. *Time for drastic action!*

He went into the bathroom, put the bathtub plug in, turned on the faucets and threw in a little bit of bubble bath for good measure. Then he went back into the bedroom and spoke with authority. "Okay, little brother, on your feet!"

Keegan threw back the covers. Lewis groaned and pulled them back on again. Just as quickly, Keegan had them pulled off again. He laughed. "Hey, remember, I'm still bigger than you."

Lewis glared up at his brother.

"C'mon," Keegan said. "A hot bath will feel really good on your sore muscles and bruises. Trust me on this one."

"It's a bit more than just sore muscles," Lewis said through gritted teeth.

Nonetheless, he slowly hauled himself up off the bed. He grabbed onto the crib and then the doorframe for support as he slowly made his way to the bathroom.

Keegan went ahead of him and turned off the bathwater then went back into the bedroom and got some clothes for Lewis. He chose a warm sweatshirt and a comfortable looking old pair of jeans.

Lewis had managed to get his shirt off by the time Keegan got back.

It was the first time that Keegan had really seen the extent of

Lewis's injuries. For a moment, he was too angry for words.

Lewis glanced up and saw him, and rightly understood his reaction.

Keegan felt anger slowly give way to compassion. "They really did a number on you," he said gruffly.

Lewis nodded and smiled weakly.

"Are you sure you don't want to go to the Health Center?"

Lewis shook his head. "Not much they can do."

Keegan felt anger returning. "You should press charges. We could get those creeps behind bars!"

Lewis shook his head again.

Keegan didn't have the heart to keep badgering him. "I'll get you some more of those pain pills that Joshua dropped off."

He brought Lewis a glass of water and watched as he swallowed the tablets. "There's some hot coffee waiting for you," he said, "and I'll make some bacon and eggs and toast."

"No, it's okay..." Lewis started to protest.

"And an easy chair," Keegan promised.

Lewis nodded wearily and Keegan closed the door and went to start breakfast.

He made sure the fire was going good, too and the small house was warming up nicely by the time Lewis made his way out of the bathroom.

And he did look marginally better.

Keegan had decided to make a bacon and egg sandwich for his brother so it would be easier for him to eat sitting in the easy chair. He pushed a footstool over and helped him swing his legs up onto it. Lewis hadn't managed to get his socks on. Keegan put them on for him before handing Lewis a cup of coffee.

Lewis took a sip and smiled up at him. "Thanks," he said.

Keegan sighed in relief. He hadn't realized before just how worried he'd been about Lewis. But if his brother could still manage a smile, then maybe things were going to be all right after all.

Keegan had made a sandwich and coffee for himself as well and he decided to eat with Lewis in the living room. He had a good view of the lake from where he sat on the couch. It was going to be a beautiful day. The sun was shining out over the lake, sparkling on the thin ice.

Keegan commented on the warm sunshine and added, "A few good days of this and we'll be able to put our boat in the water."

"Yeah," Lewis responded but his voice lacked enthusiasm.

He'd eaten all of his sandwich though and even agreed to a second cup of coffee. Keegan cleaned up the kitchen and poured himself another cup as well. He glanced at his watch. It was almost nine o'clock.

He sat down on the edge of the couch. "Randi was hoping I'd go to church with her…" he began tentatively.

"You should go," Lewis said.

"I don't like to leave you alone."

"It's okay." Lewis smiled sadly. "Maybe Starla and Karissa will come home today."

Keegan nodded, wishing he knew more about what was going on. Last time, Starla had just slipped right back into their lives almost as if she'd never been gone. But he supposed, even someone as patient as Lewis could finally get tired of it all.

As if in answer to his thoughts, Lewis added, "I don't know what we're going to do, Starla and I. It's—going to be more difficult this time."

"Just take it slow," Keegan advised. "Be honest with yourself and with her. It's important that she knows the effect that her actions have had on you and on Karissa. Maybe that's what's different this time. Maybe she's getting an idea of some of the consequences of her actions—like that you got beat up."

Lewis was starting to look depressed again and Keegan decided to shift the topic a little. "So Randi and Chance and I will probably cruise in here after church. We'll make you lunch and maybe I'll even do the dishes again!"

Lewis nodded and made another attempt at a smile.

Keegan stood to his feet. "Do you want the TV on before I go? Or maybe the radio or some music?"

Lewis shook his head. "I don't know."

Keegan wandered over to the CD player that was on the kitchen counter. A CD was lying beside it. The title track was "You" and the band was "The Kry."

"What's this one?" he asked, holding it up for Lewis to see.

"Colin dropped it by a few days ago," Lewis replied in the same weary voice. "He said that it had helped him to get through a tough time and I guess he thought maybe it would help me, too."

"Would you like me to put it on for you?" Keegan asked.

Lewis shrugged. "I don't care."

"Well, maybe I'll put it on."

Lewis shrugged again and turned away.

Keegan put the CD on but also put the remote control by Lewis's chair in case he wanted to turn it off later.

He hated to be leaving him. But he looked okay…

"You know my cell phone number…"

Lewis rolled his eyes and grinned. "Yeah, yeah. Now get out of here."

Keegan relaxed a little. Maybe Lewis would be all right after all.

And he was anxious to get home to his family. He wanted to see the look on Chance's face when they gave him the big blue teddy bear. It was almost bigger than the little boy himself but it was soft and cuddly too. Keegan knew that Chance would love it.

AFTER ALL, LEWIS WAS GLAD that Keegan had turned on the music. It would have been way too quiet all of a sudden otherwise.

But even with the music, Lewis was beginning to feel depression weighing him down once again.

The first song on the CD didn't help matters much. "I can't stop thinking about you" was a line that was often repeated and it took a while for Lewis to shift gears and realize that the writer was talking about the Lord Jesus.

The person who Lewis "couldn't stop thinking about" was Starla. Every waking moment—and some of his sleeping ones too!—were consumed with thoughts of her.

Maybe he should get his mind on the Lord... After all, it was Easter. Lewis picked up his Bible. Part of the program at Goldrock Camp was to read through the Bible in a year, and Lewis and Starla had begun together in January.

Lewis started where he'd left off two days before, but as he tried to read about the Old Testament kings, the words became a blur. The CD was still playing. Now, the lyrics were "you're all I need; you're all I want" and once again, Lewis's thoughts flew to Starla.

He pointed the remote towards the CD player and pressed the "stop" button. Silence descended on the room.

And with it, the now familiar overwhelming sense of aloneness.

Everyone would be at church.

Celebrating, singing, praising the Lord together on Resurrection Sunday—families, friends—together.

Lewis tried to shake his thoughts free again. He couldn't—wouldn't—give in to the despair that was threatening to pull him down. He knew how hard it was to come back up from those dark depths. He'd almost not made it back that time when his mom had died.

He'd felt the same sense of aloneness then.

He clicked on the CD again. But he flipped past the first few songs. Maybe something towards the end…

Suddenly, it was as if Jesus himself was speaking personally to him. The song began: "I know there are times your dreams turn to dust. You wonder as you cry why it has to hurt so much…"

Lewis sat back and let the words sweep over his soul.

> I know there are times
> Your dreams turn to dust
> You wonder as you cry
> Why it has to hurt so much
> Give me all your sadness
> Someday you will know the reason why
> With a child–like heart
> Simply put your trust in Me.
>
> Take My hand and walk where I lead
> Keep your eyes on Me alone
> Don't you say why were the old days better
> Just because you're scared of the unknown
> Take My hand and walk.

Don't live in the past
Cause yesterday's gone
Wishing memories would last
You're afraid to carry on
You don't know what's comin'
But you know the one who holds tomorrow
I will be your guide
Take you through the night
If you keep your eyes on Me.

Take My hand and walk where I lead
Keep your eyes on me alone
Don't you say why were the old days better
Just because you're scared of the unknown
Take my hand and walk where I lead
You will never be alone
Faith is to be sure of what you hope for
And the evidence of things unseen
So take my hand and walk.

Just like a child
Holding daddy's hand
Don't let go of me
You know you can't stand
On your own.

Take my hand and walk where I lead
Keep your eyes on me alone
Don't you say why were the old days better
Just because you're scared of the unknown
Take My hand and walk.

Lewis looked up and saw a picture on the wall that Missy had taken of Karissa and him walking down a tree-lined pathway.

"Just like a child holding daddy's hand…"

Lewis knew that's what he needed to do—just hold onto the Heavenly Father's hand.

He clicked off the CD and opened his Bible again. This time, he turned to the Gospels. He would read about the resurrection—how Jesus had overcome death and the grave.

But once again the familiar words seem to blur together. He knew about Jesus' trial before the governor and how the crowd had cried out for His death. The same crowd who just days before had treated Him like a celebrity. Now they were calling for His death by crucifixion—the most horrible method invented by men to kill each other.

Suddenly, the words leapt off the page.

"My God, my God, why did you abandon me?"

Jesus—*abandoned*—by the crowd of people—by His closest friends—by His family—and now even by the One who was closer than we could ever know or imagine—*one part of the Holy Trinity abandoning another!*

It would seem impossible except that it had actually happened.

God had loved the world so much that He'd given His only Son—Jesus.

He'd abandoned Him.

The words seemed to echo through the room.

I know what it feels like to be abandoned.

Chapter 9

But Jesus had also been the one to say, "Father, forgive them, for they don't know what they're doing."

Jesus had been able to forgive even as He was still enduring the pain and the rejection—and the abandonment.

Tears filled Lewis's eyes as he finally understood what was different this time. He'd hardened his heart against his wife.

Lewis thought back to the moment when he'd been lying beaten on the ground and Starla had been asked to choose between him and that other man.

And she had been silent!

Yes, that had been the moment when something had closed up inside of him. And he had rejected her as surely as she had rejected him.

It was the point at which he needed to begin again—to soften his heart towards her—to forgive her.

Lewis stood to his feet.

All the confusion and darkness was gone now.

He knew what he had to do.

He was determined to go and see Starla at that very moment.

But it was an effort even to put his boots on.

And not for the first time, Lewis wished that he had some kind of vehicle. He didn't regret spending his money on fixing up the house and on things for Starla and Karissa. And most of the time, they hadn't minded the long walk to the lodge. But today, he knew it was going to be a real challenge.

He thought about calling Keegan but knew that he would be in church. And he wanted to see Starla alone anyway.

He was pretty sure that she wouldn't have gone to church. But if she had, he would just wait at the lodge for her.

As Lewis headed towards the door, he saw the toy that he'd been going to give Karissa for Easter. It was a set of bright yellow rubber ducks—a mother duck with a place on her back where three little baby ducks could fit. Lewis knew that Karissa would enjoy playing in the tub with them. And he'd take her to the beach in the summer, too, and let her play with them there. He picked up the package and started out the door. It would be nice to have something to bring Karissa and maybe it would distract her enough so that he could talk to Starla.

The walk was harder than he could possibly have imagined.

He knew he should turn back. He was much too weak physically and the pain in his chest and shoulder grew steadily worse as he walked.

And he hadn't worn a coat. He'd thought about it briefly but knew it would require too much effort to put on. His sweatshirt had seemed warm enough when he'd first begun and all his thoughts had been concentrated on just the effort of walking on the rutted frozen ground. It was just an old hunting road that went past his house but it connected up to the community roads and it would be easier going once he got on those.

Lewis was soon wishing that he'd gone back for a coat. The wind had picked up and it was carrying the cold air from off the still frozen lake and blowing it inland. But Lewis knew that if he ever did go back, he'd never get going again.

When he reached the center of the community, there were more houses and other buildings but no people. It felt so strange. Usually there were people walking and children out running around.

But on Easter morning, the children were always given a small bag of candy after the service. And Lewis knew there was a drama planned for that morning and there would be some special music as well. The church would be packed today with both adults and children.

Only raw determination kept him going as he walked past the Community Center, the school, the daycare and the Health Center. He wanted so badly just to sit down somewhere but knew that if he did, there was no way in the world that he'd be able to stand up again.

He just had to keep going—past the Northern Store and the hockey arena and down the long road toward the old mine site. There were a couple of small roads leading off the main one but mostly there were trees and rocks and an occasional glimpse of the lake.

The temptation to stop grew stronger and stronger.

But he'd come this far.

He kept stumbling on, feeling almost disconnected from his body as he kept going—and going.

Finally, the lodge came into view. And still it seemed to take forever—walking over the crushed rocks that made up the road—a legacy of the old mine.

He would have been steadier walking on flat, smooth ground.

But he was here at last!

Still clutching the toy for Karissa, Lewis made his way to the front door and fumbled with the doorknob.

It was locked!

It couldn't be!

Lewis summoned strength that he didn't know he had and knocked on the door. They must have all gone to church—everyone—even Starla.

He'd have to wait for them. He couldn't—he just couldn't—go one step further.

Karissa had woken up early and had eaten an early breakfast so she was hungry again by eleven o'clock. Starla didn't think Missy would mind that she made her daughter a sandwich and got her some juice. Karissa had just finished eating, and Starla was lifting her out of the chair when there was a knock on the door.

She began automatically to walk towards the door with Karissa in her arms, when she suddenly realized that it could be her father! He could easily enough have found out that she was staying at the lodge.

The knock wasn't repeated which only served to make Starla more nervous. She hoped that Joshua had made sure that every door was locked before he left. Maybe she should call the police right away.

But maybe no one was there. It had sounded like a knock but maybe it had been something else—a branch brushing against the wall—or maybe a woodpecker on a tree nearby.

She went towards the huge windows that fronted the building. If she could just look at the right angle, she could see who was at the door.

Her heart flew to her throat. *Lewis!*

Quickly, she rushed to the door and unlocked it.

"Lewis…"

"Daddy!"

He was leaning up against the wall by the door, looking as if the slightest breeze would knock him over.

Starla set Karissa down and reached out an arm towards him. She was glad she had hold of him as Karissa wrapped her arms around his leg, throwing him off balance.

"Be careful," Starla said as she saw Lewis wince.

But Karissa had seen the new toy in Lewis's hand and rightly guessed that it was for her. She released his leg and reached for the clear plastic bag with the rubber ducks visible within.

Lewis let go of the bag when she tugged on it and as she was happily gurgling and clutching her new toy, Starla helped Lewis in through the door. Karissa toddled in after them and Starla locked the door again.

Every step seemed to be an effort for him. "When did you last have some of your pain pills?" Starla asked.

"I don't know," Lewis mumbled. "This morning sometime."

She led him to a chair and quickly rushed off to find something for him. She looked in the bathroom cabinet, didn't find anything and then ran into the kitchen, flinging each cupboard door open until she found a bottle of extra–strength Tylenol. She shook two out, replaced the bottle and poured Lewis a glass of water.

As she handed him the glass, she felt his cold hand. Then she noticed… "You don't have a jacket on! How far did you walk?"

"From home," Lewis murmured in a barely audible voice.

"Come by the fire," she said, helping him to his feet. "Joshua lit it this morning."

Karissa followed behind them, shaking the package as she went, trying to shake the rubber ducks loose.

Starla didn't try to talk anymore. It was taking everything they both had to walk the length of the room.

Lewis dropped down onto the sofa, still looking as if he would topple over any minute.

"Maybe you should lie down," Starla said.

Lewis mumbled some sort of assent as Starla pulled off his boots, and with a stifled groan, he eased down onto the couch, resting his head on the cushion she'd set there. There was a blanket draped over the back; Starla pulled it down and arranged it over top of Lewis.

Karissa was getting more anxious to open her package. She started to hit Lewis on the chest with it. "Da, Da…" she said insistently.

Starla grabbed it quickly out of her hand. "I'll help you!" She tore the bag open in one swift movement. "I'm sorry," she said breathlessly to Lewis.

He looked intently up at her and spoke with an unexpected fervency, "I forgive you."

Starla suddenly felt all the strength go out of her. She dropped to her knees beside him.

"I came to tell you," he said.

Tears filled her eyes and for a moment, she couldn't speak. Then she managed finally in a shaky voice to say the one word, "Thanks."

It was Karissa who lightened the mood, setting each of the little ducks up on the couch between them. "Da, Da…" she said.

"Duck…" Lewis said enunciating the word carefully for her.

"Du…"

"Du—*ck*," he said again, this time emphasizing the last sound in the word.

"Du—*ck*," Karissa carefully imitated.

Lewis grinned broadly. "That's right—duck." He shifted his gaze towards Starla again. "Did you hear her? She said 'duck'."

"Yes, I heard her." Starla smiled back at him. Then she turned towards her daughter and showed her how to put the baby ducks onto the mother's saucer–shaped back. Karissa gurgled with pleasure as she saw how the three small ducks fit snuggly together there.

As Karissa methodically took each of the ducks off and put them back on again, she constantly repeated her new word, "Duck… duck… duck…"

Starla glanced at Lewis, saw his eyes glowing with pride and joy, and followed his gaze back to Karissa.

A measure of contentment filled her soul and Starla wished that this one moment could last forever.

But Karissa was starting to get sleepy. She paused in her game to yawn and rub her eyes. Lewis lifted his arm to gently rub her back. "You getting tired, sweetie?" he asked.

Karissa looked up at him with drooping eyes for a moment then crawled up onto the couch. Lewis pulled the blanket over her as she snuggled down beside him.

The toy ducks had fallen off the couch in the process. Karissa put out her hand for them and looked beseechingly at Starla.

She picked them up off the floor, setting the baby ducks onto the mother's back. Karissa laid her hand over them, closed her eyes and promptly fell asleep.

Lewis and Starla exchanged glances over her head.

"I don't remember her falling asleep that easily before," Starla said.

Lewis smiled. "She doesn't usually."

"She was up early this morning. And yesterday was…" Starla's voice trailed off. No, she didn't want to talk about yesterday.

"It's okay," Lewis said gently. "We have today."

Starla smiled through her tears, feeling a well of love and gratitude for this kind and generous man—her husband.

But the past days' events were catching up with him as well. With a final tired smile, he closed his eyes and fell asleep almost as fast as Karissa had.

Starla remained where she was on the floor beside the couch, content just to watch them.

She had almost dozed off herself when there was a noise at the front door. She could hear Joshua and Keegan—and then Missy.

They seemed to be upset about something and as she listened, Starla began to understand why.

"I don't think he could have gone far," Joshua said.

"I'd like to organize a search party right away," Keegan said anxiously. "I should never have left him."

"You didn't know," Missy tried to reassure him.

"I knew he was depressed," Keegan said, sounding angry with himself.

"I'll get hold of Colin," Joshua said. "We'll get everyone to meet at the Community Center."

Starla knew she had to say something—and quickly.

She stood to her feet. They were huddled in an anxious group close to the front door. Randi and her baby, Chance, were with them also.

They noticed her right away and she walked quickly towards them.

"He's here," she said. "Lewis is over on the couch—asleep."

Keegan didn't wait for her to finish speaking. He ran the length of the room as the others followed close behind.

Starla didn't see the look on his face but she saw him sway and reach out to grab the arm of the couch. His breath was coming in deep shuddering gasps and when he turned towards her, she saw tears in his eyes.

"How did he get here?" he asked in a voice thick with emotion.

"He walked," Starla said quietly, still afraid of waking Lewis or Karissa.

"He walked!" Keegan's voice trembled and he sank down into a chair. "He should have called me."

Karissa whimpered softly and moved her arm, sending the rubber ducks thumping to the floor. The sound woke her up a little bit more and she rolled over, sending her knees crashing into Lewis's chest. As she heard him groan, Starla rushed over to them and swept Karissa up into her arms.

As she walked away from the couch, she rocked her daughter and spoke comforting words. "Shh, shh, go back to sleep now. It's okay."

"Mommy?" the sleepy voice asked.

"Yes, honey, Mommy's here. It's okay."

Karissa snuggled down onto Starla's shoulder and was soon in a deep sleep once more. She didn't wake at all as Starla carried her up the stairs and set her down into a crib.

Starla stood looking down at her for a moment. She hadn't realized how much she'd missed her daughter until she was back and saw her again.

Karissa looked so sweet lying there with her lovely dark lashes and little rosebud mouth and her tiny hand curled up under her chin, She was smiling in her sleep and Starla remembered she'd done that even as a newborn. *My precious little girl...*

Suddenly, she heard Lewis cry out. Starla hurried out of the room, closing the door behind her. She looked over the balcony and saw that Keegan and Joshua were sitting on the couch with Lewis, trying unsuccessfully to calm him down.

He was crying and talking incoherently. As Starla raced down the spiral staircase, she caught a few words but they didn't make much sense. It was something about dreaming and being awake and Starla and Karissa…

"Lewis!" Starla ran towards him.

He stared at her as if he couldn't believe she was really there.

Joshua stood up quickly so Starla could take his place.

Lewis clung to her as if he'd never let her go again and Starla wrapped her arms tightly around him as well, unsure of what else to do or say that would help.

"If I'm asleep, I don't ever want to wake up again," he whispered hoarsely. "If I'm awake, I don't ever want to sleep again."

Starla smiled tremulously. "You're awake," she said.

"But you should be asleep," Keegan spoke sternly from beside him. "You don't get these waking dreams unless you're really, really tired."

Starla pulled away from him slightly. Keegan was right; he should sleep.

"No!" Lewis clung even tighter. "Don't let go yet—please."

"I won't," she said gently. "And I won't leave you again. I'll stay right here while you sleep. I just went to put Karissa to bed. I won't leave you again."

"Promise me…" But his words were slurred and she could feel him growing heavier in her arms. "Promise…"

Starla glanced over at Keegan. It was as if he was waiting for her answer even though his brother was now asleep.

But she couldn't promise to never leave. *She was planning to leave the very next day.*

"Could you help me?" she asked, avoiding his eyes as she began to lower Lewis back down onto the pillow.

Keegan gently lifted Lewis's legs up onto the couch and straightened the blanket over him again.

Starla eased her arm out from under Lewis and he cried out in his sleep.

Starla quickly reassured him, holding tightly to his hand and stroking his forehead as she murmured, "Shh, shh, it's okay now. It's okay."

She waited until his breathing was deep and even before shifting herself into a more comfortable position. She sat with crossed legs, facing towards the head of the couch with one of her arms draped over Lewis and the other holding his hand. It was a position she could maintain for quite a while and she was determined to stay with him this time, no matter how long he slept.

"I made you a sandwich."

Missy's voice startled her. All her thoughts had been on Lewis.

Starla looked up at Missy then glanced quickly around. Joshua and Keegan were both gone.

"And there's a glass of juice, too…"

But Starla didn't want to move at all, afraid that she would wake Lewis.

Missy seemed to understand. "It's okay," she said. "You can move one of your hands away."

Starla looked doubtfully up at her as Missy continued. "Joshua used to have night terrors. As long as you keep some physical contact with him, it'll be okay. Here, try moving your right hand. Okay, rub his back a little. Let him know you're still there…"

He had stirred a little when she'd moved her hand. But he was breathing deeply and evenly again now.

Missy kept her voice low. "It's really important that you drink something so you don't get dehydrated again."

Starla nodded and accepted the glass of orange juice from Missy.

She took a few swallows and set the glass down on the coffee table. "I didn't know…" She faltered, looked up at Missy, saw compassion in her eyes and continued haltingly. "I didn't know that he cared so much—about whether I was gone or not."

Missy came to sit beside Starla on the floor. There was just enough room for her to lean against the head of the couch and not have her knees quite touching Starla's.

They could talk quieter now—almost in whispers. But the move closer had also shifted the level of intimacy in the conversation. Missy wasn't the camp director's wife looking down, counseling her; she was a friend listening and confiding.

"Lewis loves you very much," she said.

The words, softly spoken, crashed like a tidal wave over Starla, leaving her struggling for breath. She shook her head, trying to keep back the flood of emotions. She didn't want to cry. If she started to cry, she'd never stop…

"I don't deserve…" Her voice broke.

"None of us deserves love," Missy said gently. "It's a gift, freely given."

"Why?" Starla spoke in a trembling voice, tears filling her eyes.

Missy smiled. "I don't know why. I guess it's a God–thing."

Yes, a God–thing—something above and beyond human understanding.

"He was always there for me," Starla said softly. "Even when we were kids—I could always count on him, you know."

Missy nodded. There were a few tears in her eyes now, too.

"He used to do drugs but when he saw that I was starting to, he quit and helped me to quit, too. And when he got Christianity, he wanted me to have that, too." Starla shook her head. "There's still some stuff I don't really get, you know. Like why Jesus had to die—I don't get that."

Missy smiled. "It's what we've been talking about—love. He did it because He loved us."

"But it seems like a funny way to show it—doesn't it? I mean, why not a hug or a gift?"

"Or a sacrifice," Missy suggested. "Sometimes, when we love someone, we're willing to give up everything for them—even our lives."

Starla shook her head again. "I don't think I know what love is."

Missy said gently, "What Lewis has for you, that's love."

Starla lowered her eyes. "I always thought he just felt sorry for me."

"You thought I felt sorry for you!"

His loud exclamation startled her and left her speechless.

How long had he been listening?

"The most beautiful woman in the world wants to marry me..." he continued, raising himself up on one elbow. "And you think—you really think I did it because I felt sorry for you!"

Starla lowered her eyes. "I was five months pregnant..." Her voice trailed off into a faint whisper "...with another man's child."

Lewis sighed deeply and put his head back down again. "I always wished that Karissa had been mine. I guess I've always thought of her that way. I was there right from her birth. I've always loved her."

And I'm going to take her away from you tomorrow!

Unaware of what Starla was thinking, Lewis continued in a tender voice. "I've always felt it was a privilege to be her father—and to be your husband."

Starla turned away again. "I don't deserve."

"It's not about deserving!" Lewis stated emphatically. "It's about loving you." His voice became tender again. "And it's about wanting to spend the rest of my life with you."

She couldn't look at him.

"Starla!" She could hear the rising panic in his voice. "Starla—what aren't you telling me?"

She winced at the pain she saw in his eyes. But he had to know. It was only a matter of time. "I'm leaving on the first plane out tomorrow."

Chapter 10

Starla bowed her head, not wanting to see how much her words had hurt him. But in the ensuing silence, she looked up again.

Her words hadn't just hurt him. *They'd killed him.*

If she didn't see his chest steadily rising and falling, she might have thought that he had actually died.

All of his life and vitality had been drained away. He was staring at the coffee table with unseeing eyes.

"Lewis…" she whispered cautiously.

He didn't move at all.

Then just his lips moved, forming careful words. "Maybe, we'll be better off without you. Just stay gone this time. It's too hard on Karissa."

Starla groaned inwardly, realizing too late how a small mistake was going to cause even greater devastation. She should have said *we're* leaving on the first plane—not *I'm* leaving on the first plane!

Starla wondered if she should wait to tell him.

But he had to know. She had been planning to pack that evening. She wasn't ever coming back—and neither was Karissa.

"I'm taking her with me."

The effect of her words was immediate and dramatic. Lewis struggled to his feet and shouted down at her in a voice thick with emotion. "No, you're not! You're not taking her! I'm not going to let you take her!"

Starla scooted back a little. It was the first time he'd ever raised his voice to her. It frightened her, like nothing else could have.

"You don't have custody," she said quietly. "You can't stop me."

He was crying openly now and trembling with rage—or grief. "You can't take her!" he yelled again and again. "You can't take her!"

They had been alone before. But everyone was back now.

Starla scrambled to her feet and Joshua stepped between her and Lewis.

Lewis fell back onto the couch with a groan then leaned forward, his body suddenly racked with the uncontrollable sobs of a person recently bereaved.

"Couldn't you have waited to tell him?" Missy demanded.

Joshua and Keegan turned towards her also. Joshua's eyes only held sadness but Keegan looked furious!

"What's going on?" he demanded.

Starla took a step backwards.

She heard Karissa start to cry. The sound of their voices must have carried through the walls. She was about to go but saw that Randi was heading up towards the nursery with Chance in her arms. Starla turned her attention back to the more urgent problem—Keegan!

Joshua was still placed strategically between them. He began a valiant attempt at trying to explain to Keegan why Starla felt she had to go. "She doesn't feel that Rabbit Lake is a safe place for her and her daughter…"

But Keegan was much too angry to hear what he had to say.

"So you're going to leave him again!" Keegan shouted. "And you think you're gonna take my niece with you?"

"She's not legally your—"

"Starla!" Joshua spun around to face her. "Missy," he said in a trembling voice. "Missy, maybe you and Starla should go check on Karissa."

Starla allowed Missy to lead her away. As they climbed the stairs, Starla expected to hear Keegan's angry voice following her but the only sound that reached her ears was Lewis's more subdued but still heart-breaking sobs.

She glanced down over the railing and saw that the two men were sitting on either side of Lewis again. They each had a hand on one of his shoulders and Joshua seemed to be praying.

In the nursery, Randi was holding both children on her lap and sitting in the rocking chair. Karissa had obviously been crying; her eyes were red and her cheeks looked flushed. As soon as she saw Starla, she called out "Mommy!" and began to cry again.

Starla couldn't help noticing Randi's angry look as she took Karissa from her. "You're leaving again," she said.

Tears filled Starla's eyes. *She had to go! For Karissa's sake, she had to go!* She began to walk around the room, rocking the little girl and speaking soothing words to her.

"Starla…" Missy said tentatively.

She didn't want to talk to anyone!

"Is it okay if I tell Randi why you need to go?"

Starla shrugged as if it didn't matter. But as Missy began to speak, her heart started to beat faster and faster…

The words sounded so matter-of-fact: "Starla's father has been sexually abusing her since she was a baby. Now Starla has good reason to believe that Karissa might be in danger from him as well."

She couldn't breathe! And the room was beginning to spin around!

Missy slipped Karissa out of her arms and Randi helped her to sit down in the rocking chair.

Her breath returned in a huge trembling sob.

She felt comforting hands—heard a comforting voice.

It took her a minute to realize that she was alone with Randi. Missy had taken the two children out of the room.

"I'm sorry," Randi said softly, "I didn't know."

It felt so good to have someone understand!

"I don't want to leave him…" Starla said in a voice still thick with tears.

"You shouldn't have to," Randi said in a hard, determined voice.

Starla shook her head. "I don't see any other way."

"There is a way," Randi said firmly. She walked towards the door. "You okay to have the kids in again?"

"Yeah, I'm so sorry. I shouldn't have started to cry like that."

"It's okay," Randi replied shortly.

She opened the door. Missy had been out on the balcony with the children. She came in, heading immediately over to a corner of the room, engaging the children with toys to distract them from the turmoil going on around them.

"This is so hard on her," Starla said, her eyes on Karissa.

"It'd have been worse if you'd just let things go on," Randi said darkly. "You made the right decision for your daughter. You're just going about it in the wrong way."

Starla wanted to challenge her on that point but Missy spoke first. "Joshua and Keegan are on their way up."

Starla shook her head. She couldn't face them just now. She couldn't. And she didn't want any more yelling or crying around her daughter. "No..." she said.

But Missy hadn't given much advanced warning and Keegan was in the room before she could say another word.

And he didn't waste any time before speaking. "I'm sorry," he said and sounded as if he meant it. But he had more on his mind. "Starla, what your father did wasn't just wrong—it was against the law."

Yes, that's what Joshua had said.

"You know that as a police officer, I can't ignore this information."

Starla lowered her eyes. "Maybe he shouldn't have told you."

"You'd give up your home!" Keegan almost shouted the words but lowered his voice when Karissa turned frightened eyes in his direction. "You'd destroy Lewis," he continued in a quieter but still intense voice. "You'd take your daughter away from the only father she's ever known. You'd do all that to protect a man who doesn't even deserve to be called your father?"

Starla gazed up at him in confusion.

She was protecting her father?

"No," she declared, her thoughts clearing. "I'm protecting myself. And I'm protecting Karissa... by moving away."

Keegan crouched down beside the rocking chair. "Starla," he said with a burning intensity in his eyes and in his voice, "you're not the one who should have to move."

Starla felt more confused than ever.

Joshua stepped forward. "Your father should be in jail, Starla."

She shook her head. "He's been in jail before. He always comes out again in a few weeks, a few months, a couple of years.

But always—always—they let him come home for Christmas. And other times…"

"There'd be no more of that," Keegan said firmly. "For one thing, there will be a restraining order on him. He won't be allowed any contact with you or with Karissa."

Joshua said, "He's right, Starla. Your father should be in prison, not you."

She didn't at first understand what he meant. But the house in Winnipeg had been like a prison in many ways. There was a certain feeling of safety and of being sheltered and protected as one of "Eric's Girls" but in many ways she had been like a prisoner there, resigned to her fate.

"I'll need to ask you a few questions," Keegan began in a more official tone.

"No, no, I can't!" Starla stood to her feet and began pacing around the room. "He'd be so angry. And Gookum too… I can't! I can't!"

"Starla…" Joshua began in a gentle voice.

She whirled around to face him. "You shouldn't have told him!"

"I had to," Joshua declared. "Even though you're married and have a child, you're still just eighteen years old. And you've been part of our program here." He shook his head. "Even if I thought I didn't have a moral obligation, I'd have a legal obligation to report this."

Starla sank down onto the rocking chair again. "Will I have to testify in court—with him there—and my Grandma—and a bunch of other people?"

"You won't be alone, Starla," Randi said. "We'll all be there with you."

"And what if the judge says he's not guilty—or if my Grandma puts up bail money. She did that once and he was out for a long time before the trial…"

"There will be a 'no–contact provision' even if he does manage to get out on bail," Keegan said. "He won't be able to make contact with you and we can extend that to include Lewis and Karissa as well. But I don't think he'll get off too lightly. He's a repeat offender and I have an idea the judge might just give him the maximum sentence this time."

Starla felt a tiny spark of hope. *Was it really possible to be free after all these years?*

She was afraid to ask—but she had to know. "How—how long is the maximum sentence?"

"If he had sexual intercourse with you—fourteen years."

Fourteen years! Fourteen years!

Time enough for Karissa to grow up—to have a normal childhood!

Time enough for her and Lewis to build a home—a happy, healthy home.

Starla jumped to her feet. She had to talk to Lewis!

"I'll do it," she said over her shoulder to Keegan as she scooped up her daughter and headed out the door.

She almost flew down the stairs.

Karissa caught sight of Lewis sitting on the couch and called out, "Daddy!"

Lewis turned slowly towards them. He still looked emotionally beaten down. But he smiled cautiously and then stretched out his hand towards her.

Starla gave a small cry and ran the rest of the way into his arms.

Lewis hugged her tightly. Karissa standing beside them on the couch, jumped up and down, giggling happily as her parents embraced.

"You should have told me," Lewis said gently.

"I was afraid."

Lewis pulled away a little. "Of me?"

"No," Starla said softly. "I was afraid of my father—and my grandma."

"Duck! Duck!" Karissa called out.

Starla smiled and bent to pick up the rubber ducks from where they'd fallen. The little girl laughed, sat down beside them and began to play, taking the ducks off the mother's back—and then putting them on again.

Starla tucked her legs up and leaned her head on Lewis's shoulder, snuggling in close beside him. Karissa continued to play, smiling up at them occasionally and saying her new word over and over again. "Duck! Duck!"

Starla moved her head a little to smile up at Lewis and was alarmed to see that his face was twisted in pain. "Am I hurting you?" she gasped, starting to move away. She'd been leaning on him, not on his broken collarbone but on the opposite shoulder. Still, she shouldn't be putting any pressure at all on his chest.

"No, you're not hurting me."

But he was so obviously in pain. "Can I get you some Tylenol or something?"

Lewis smiled weakly. "No." He wrapped both of his arms around her, drawing her close once again.

Now she couldn't see his face. She could only hear his voice.

"I was just thinking about Karissa—and you."

Starla stayed with her head on his shoulder. Maybe it was easier for him to talk if she wasn't looking at him.

"She's so happy…"

Starla could see that she was happy. It was amazing how long she could play the one game. A young child could find joy in such little things.

"No one's ever hurt her," Lewis continued. "…Not like you were hurt."

His voice was shaking now. Each word seemed an effort. "I wish—I wish I could go back and change things for you—give you a mom and dad who would love you and—and keep you safe."

Starla reached up to touch his cheek. It was wet with tears.

He was crying—*for her!*

And, in that moment, for the first time in her entire life, Starla *knew* that somebody loved her.

He didn't just feel sorry for her. He wasn't doing it as a Christian duty. And he especially wasn't like the other men—or her father—"loving" her only as long as she was of some use to them.

No, this man, this good, kind man *loved her*—just loved her—not wanting anything in return.

No, that wasn't completely true.

He wanted her love in return.

"I love you," she said softly.

It took a moment before he could reply in a voice that trembled a little. "Thank you." Then in a steadier voice, he said, "I love you, too."

Starla pulled away a little to look up into his eyes. "I know."

More tears followed—this time in her eyes as well.

They clung tightly to each other, neither wanting to ever let go again.

But someone else was starting to feel left out. The rubber ducks had finally lost their interest. "Daddy—Mommy—Daddy—

Mommy…"

Karissa was bouncing up and down on the soft couch cushions and trying to climb on top of Lewis.

Starla let go of Lewis to pick up her daughter. "Hey, no jumping on Daddy yet," she said, pulling her over onto her lap instead.

She took Karissa's hand and gently touched Lewis's chest. "Daddy has *owwie*. We have to be *gentle*."

Karissa's eyes grew wide with concern as she looked up at Lewis and tenderly asked, "Owwie?"

Lewis smiled down at her, looking as if he might cry again then he put his arm around Starla, encircling them both.

A deep peace settled over her. She could hear sounds in the distance, people working in the kitchen, talking, moving pots and pans around, a chair being scraped back, more voices…

It all seemed so far away—almost in a different time and place.

For right here and now, there was just Lewis and Karissa and her—the three of them on a tiny island safe and sheltered from the rest of the world.

Chapter 11

Karissa and Starla had both fallen asleep in his arms and Lewis was starting to doze off as well when Missy came over to ask them if they would like to eat dinner.

Lewis looked up, startled. "What time is it?" he asked groggily.

"It's only four o'clock," Missy answered, "but some of us didn't really eat lunch so we thought we'd have an early supper."

Starla and Karissa were both waking up at the sound of their voices.

"We'll be right there," Lewis said.

It was still difficult moving around and Lewis was glad for Starla's support as they walked towards the group already assembling around a large table.

It was actually three of the smaller tables pushed together to make one long table where all of them could sit. There were places for the two children as well, Chance in a high chair and Karissa on a booster seat.

Missy was just carrying in a plate with sliced ham and another with sliced moose meat on it. Randi followed her with a big bowl of mashed potatoes. There was other food on the table as well. As a matter of fact, there was a lot of food! And the table was all decorated up fancy with candles and a white tablecloth and everything.

Then Lewis remembered—Easter!

They'd gone to a lot of work—and in such a short amount of time, too.

Lewis smiled. It did seem appropriate though, that on this special day of celebrating Jesus' resurrection, Lewis would also be able to celebrate the new relationship he had with Starla. It was almost as if she had been dead and come back to him.

Lewis reached over and took Starla's hand on his right and Karissa's on his left as Joshua smiled and said, "Let's thank the Lord for this wonderful feast."

Joshua did thank the Lord for the food but also prayed for Starla and Lewis and Karissa that God would help them through this difficult time.

After the prayer, Keegan said, "There's a warrant out for Garby's arrest now and I have a search warrant for Yvonne's house, too."

Lewis noticed then for the first time that Keegan was wearing his uniform.

Keegan grinned at him. "I was working while you three were dozing off on the couch there."

Lewis looked quickly back at Starla. *Would she be upset to hear there were warrants out already? Were things moving too fast for her?*

She did look a little nervous but not because things were moving too fast. "I just wish it was all over," she said.

"It soon will be," Keegan assured her.

"I stopped by and got your bottle of pain medication, too," Keegan added. "You must really be needing some by now."

"It's not too bad," Lewis said, not liking to be the centre of attention. "Starla found me some Tylenol this morning."

"Well, better take some now," Keegan advised.

Lewis obliged, thankful that his brother had brought them over. The pain was pretty much constant and the pills did take a bit of the edge off.

Missy began to pass the plates then and soon everyone was eating and the conversation was limited to how good the food was. And could someone please pass the salt…

They were almost finished their meal when suddenly there was a noise at the front door.

And Garby Quill strode in, looking as if he owned the place!

"Hey, little brother, you forgot to invite me to this family gathering!"

Joshua flicked his eyes in Lewis's direction and moved his chin slightly towards the kitchen.

Lewis got the message loud and clear! He'd been thinking the same thing.

But Starla seemed frozen in place, staring wide–eyed at her father.

Fortunately, there were others to help. Missy scooped Karissa up while Lewis whispered urgently in Starla's ear, "Let's go!"

Once moving, Starla was suddenly in a hurry and Lewis found himself behind her as they rushed into the kitchen, heading towards the back bedroom, which had a lock on the door.

Garby's booming voice followed after them. "Hey, whatcha runnin' away for? I just came to see my granddaughter. I've got a right to see her if I want to. Hey, what's wrong with your boyfriend, Starla? He looks like he got run over by a pulp truck."

"Don't look back!" Lewis said as Starla hesitated and began to turn around.

Her father still held so much power over her!

"You're under arrest," Keegan's voice rang out with authority.

"Hey, I had nothing to do with that. I haven't even seen the guy for a week or maybe two or three…"

Lewis couldn't believe it! Garby thought he was being arrested for beating him up! Did the man feel so little remorse for hurting his daughter that the thought never even entered his mind that he might be arrested for it!

Once in the guest bedroom, Missy handed Karissa to Starla. "I'm going to call the police station—get some back–up."

Even as he shut and locked the door, Lewis could hear Garby calling out to Starla. "C'mon baby, I just want to see you for a minute…"

Keegan or Joshua might have spoken as well. But Lewis couldn't hear them because Starla had begun to scream hysterically. She was holding Karissa tightly in her arms and running around the room like a caged animal looking for escape. Karissa's terrified cries only added to the general noise and confusion.

Lewis tried to speak calmly to his wife. He could hear a scuffle outside the door then something loudly thumped against the wood frame. Someone rattled the door handle and Lewis heard Garby call loudly, "C'mon Starla…!"

She ran into the bathroom, still clutching her wailing daughter, and before Lewis could stop her, she had shut and locked the door.

"Starla! Starla! Let me in, please!" He rattled the door handle as he spoke.

But suddenly, he thought he sounded just like her father.

And she couldn't hear him anyway above her cries and Karissa's.

The bedroom door burst open! Lewis spun around, prepared to defend his wife and daughter, no matter what the cost.

But it was only Joshua. He had a bruise on his left cheek and a split lip.

Joshua shut the door behind him and said calmly, "There's enough of them out there now. They're reading him his rights."

Weak with relief, Lewis leaned against the bathroom door. Then he turned and knocked, keeping his voice calm as he called out, "Starla, it's okay now. Everything's okay now."

He wasn't sure if she'd heard him. Had there been some small abatement in the hysterical sobs?

Lewis knocked on the door again. "Starla, honey, it's okay. You can come out now," he said, trying to make his voice loud enough to be heard but gentle enough to be reassuring.

A police siren sounded, and with a grin, Joshua bounded towards the glass patio doors. "He's gone!" Joshua exclaimed.

Lewis almost collapsed with relief. "Thank you, God," he breathed.

And now for sure, there was a noticeable decrease in crying. "Starla, he's gone!" Lewis called through the door.

There was a sharp click, the door flew open, and then they were in his arms! Tears sprang to Lewis's eyes as he held them close, speaking words of comfort as their sobs gradually subsided into deep, calm breaths.

"Are you guys okay?" Missy's worried voice sounded from the kitchen doorway.

Lewis and Starla moved apart a little to face her but it was Joshua who responded, "We're fine, honey."

"Oh, Joshua! Your lip is bleeding and—"

"It's okay," Joshua said in a reassuring voice as he walked towards her.

"Maybe a cold cloth—or some ice…" Missy's voice faded

away as she and Joshua left the room.

Lewis smoothed back Karissa's damp curls and kissed her on the forehead. The little girl's face was flushed and her eyes drooped. "Sleepy?" he asked. Karissa reached out her arms towards him. Lewis sat down on the bed and Starla put Karissa in his lap before sitting down beside him.

"I think she has some pajamas in her bag," Starla said.

It was the first time she had spoken and her voice was hoarse from crying. Joshua hugged her close again. "Yeah, I packed some," he said past the lump in his throat.

It had been a difficult experience but now it was over. Garby had been arrested and Starla was finally free from him.

"I'll get them," Starla said, pulling away but gently kissing him on the lips before standing and walking over to where she'd left Karissa's bag.

Starla had undressed her and had her pajama bottoms on when Lewis remembered the "peek–a–boo" game they'd played before. There'd been too many tears today, he thought. It would be good to hear Karissa laugh again.

Lewis lifted the pajama top in front of his face then lowered it again and gave his very best, "Boo!"

Karissa thought it was the greatest thing and laughed joyfully as he played the game again and then again.

Lewis and Starla exchanged smiles over her head and in the brief lull, Karissa grew impatient. "Boo," she said. "Boo!" she said more insistently.

Lewis laughed. "Oh–oh, this might become her next favorite word."

Karissa proved them right. "Boo!" she said and giggled.

Missy stuck her head in. "Hot chocolate's ready if you'd like some."

"Boo!" Karissa said.

Missy laughed and said, "Boo to you, too!"

Lewis grinned. "We'll be right there."

Lewis popped the pajama top quickly over Karissa's head and she helped to push her own arms through the sleeves.

Joshua had the fire going well and Missy had brought a tray filled with mugs of hot chocolate and set it on the coffee table.

Randi must have taken her son upstairs during the confrontation between Garby and the police. She was just coming down the steps as Lewis, Starla and Karissa were getting settled on the couch.

It was cozy and comfortable sitting around the fire, sipping hot chocolate and for a moment, Lewis could almost forget the tragic events encircling their lives.

It was Missy who shattered their semblance of tranquility by saying, "Keegan called. He'll be coming over soon."

"What does he want?" Lewis demanded. If it was to give them an update on Starla's father, Lewis wished that Keegan would just stay away. He really didn't want to hear any more about that man—ever!

Missy hesitated, looking around at them. "Maybe I should wait till he gets here and he can tell you everything himself. And maybe, if the children could go up to the nursery again…"

"I don't mind," Randi spoke up quickly. She stood to her feet with her son in her arms and reached out to take Karissa as well.

"She should probably use the potty," Lewis said as Karissa readily went into her auntie's arms. "And I usually read her a story before bedtime and—"

Randi laughed. "I've put her to bed before. I know her routine."

"Yeah, I know but…" The plain fact was that he wasn't ready to let her go yet. *He'd come so close to losing her.* "Maybe, she could stay down here until Keegan comes. Or I could go with you and somebody could call me…"

Randi just smiled. "Kiss Daddy good–night," she said, leaning over so Karissa could reach Lewis. "Okay, now Mommy, too…"

Lewis resisted the urge to take the little girl into his arms instead of giving her a quick kiss and hug.

But Missy was probably right. It would be better for the children to be somewhere else if there was more bad news…

But what more could there be?

He really thought they'd all had more than enough for one day.

"Maybe we could talk to Keegan tomorrow," Lewis suggested as he watched Randi take the children up the spiral staircase.

But even as he spoke, Keegan arrived at the door. He called out a greeting to Randi before making his way towards the others.

Missy offered him some hot chocolate but he said he'd already grabbed a cup of coffee at the station.

Lewis took Starla's hand and braced himself for whatever his brother had to say. And Keegan didn't hold them in suspense for long. After finding out that Missy hadn't told them anything yet, he said, "We arrested Yvonne Quill as well."

"Why?" Starla gasped.

"Assaulting a police officer," Keegan replied grimly.

Joshua leaned forward. "You?" he asked.

"No, one of our newer officers. Kinda took him by surprise, actually."

"Anybody hurt?" Joshua asked.

Keegan shook his head.

He remained silent for a moment. He was looking at Starla.

Lewis grew nervous again. *There was more?*

"So how are you two doing?" Keegan asked with concern in his voice. "It was quite a shock having Garby show up like that." He glanced over at Joshua. "I didn't really expect him to get violent."

"He scared me," Starla answered honestly.

Lewis only nodded. He knew his brother. He was trying to decide if they could handle any more tonight or not. Lewis wanted him just to spit it out. Get it over with! Tell them the worst! And then leave them alone!

"Starla, we had a search warrant to gather evidence for your father's conviction…"

Lewis felt her draw into herself. She pulled her legs up and wrapped her arms around her chest and bowed her head.

Lewis put an arm around her, pulling her closer until she was on his lap. He held her like a child, both of his arms wrapped tightly around her. "It's okay," he said. "It's okay."

"Do you want me to continue?" Keegan asked them.

Lewis glanced down at Starla but from her new position of safety, she nodded.

"We didn't expect there to be so many…" Keegan hesitated. "Did you know that she was keeping all those clothes?"

Starla's pain–filled sob tore at Lewis's heart. "Yes," she said in a tiny voice.

"She said that they belonged to her," Keegan said heavily. "But your story matches what we found. There were clothes—mostly dresses—in every size from—baby—to—to more recent."

Lewis could see how difficult it was for Keegan to say the words but he could feel how much more difficult it was for Starla to hear them. She was trembling and he could feel her tears soaking through his shirt.

"At some point—not right now—we'll need you to identify each article and—if you can—put a date—to—to the times."

She was openly crying now and Keegan reluctantly finished what he had to say. "We'll need a blood test for matching…"

Lewis felt suddenly as if his heart had been ripped out. "What!"

"There was what appeared to be dried blood on some of the clothes—and probably other—"

"No!" Lewis exploded. "I'll kill him. I'll kill him myself. I'll kill him."

It was Starla who finally helped him to get his emotions back under control. In an instant, she went from the role of comforted to comforter, putting her arms around him, telling him that it was okay. It was okay…

But the reality of what she'd endured kept crashing in upon him over and over again. How could anyone do that to a child—a small, helpless child—a sweet, pure, innocent child? How could anyone do that to Starla—his precious wife? And for so long. Why didn't anyone see—why didn't anyone stop it?

He felt rage and then grief and then rage again.

"How come no one knew?" he demanded. "How come no one stopped it?" He glared at Joshua. "You were her uncle!"

But Joshua didn't need an accuser. He was beating himself up enough. He could barely speak and tears were running down his cheeks. "I should have kept in closer touch with Starla. I was trying to stay away. For my own protection... I'm so sorry. I didn't know… I'm so sorry…"

Missy was speaking comforting words to him. But Lewis felt no compassion—only anger—towards Joshua—and towards the whole world.

But he was especially angry at himself. *He* should have seen.

He should have known. *He* should have been able to do something to stop this horrible monstrous thing from happening to his wife—*his wife!*

Chapter 12

Lewis didn't want to know if her father had molested her after they had been married. It would kill him to know that.

But she'd still been running.

Running and still running…

She was curled up on his lap. No longer crying—just resting in his arms. Like a child who had cried herself to sleep—her cheeks were flushed and her red-rimmed eyes were closed. Lewis wondered if she *had* fallen asleep. She must be exhausted—as he was—from the emotional battering rams they'd experienced this evening.

But he had to tell her.

"I'm sorry that I wasn't a good husband to you," he said softly. "I didn't protect you. I should have found out what was wrong. I should have kept asking you till you told me why you left—why you always wanted to go away—at Christmas—on your birthday. I didn't know. But I should have found out. I should have found out somehow."

Slowly she opened her eyes and smiled gently up at him. "It's okay."

Lewis glanced around. Missy and Joshua were huddled together, their heads bowed. Keegan too, was looking down, his eyes closed. He knew they were giving Starla and him the space they needed but still staying close to offer support if it was wanted.

What he had to ask her should perhaps have been just between the two of them. But it was a knowledge he didn't want to carry alone…

"Starla… Karissa's father?"

He felt a shudder go through her body. And he wished he didn't have to ask her. Not now—after she'd been through so much.

But he had to know. "Is it your father?"

"No," she said in a small sad voice.

Then she unfolded herself from his lap and moved just a little away from him to the end of the couch. She tucked her knees up under her chin and rested her head against the back cushion.

"From the day I first got my period," Starla said matter-of-factly, "my grandma made sure that I took birth control pills. She said she didn't want to have to take care of any more mistakes. I guess she meant me and my little brother. Well, I made a 'mistake' anyway—in Winnipeg. I got sick and forgot to take my pills. The man I was with—"

She looked at Lewis with fear in her eyes.

But he wasn't about to hurt her ever again. And there was no anger or jealousy in his voice as he asked quietly, "The guy with the ponytail?"

Starla nodded and then turned away again. She didn't look at anyone else either—just straight ahead—as she continued her story. Lewis ached to take her into his arms—to comfort her. But she seemed to need to do it this way telling her story as if it had happened to someone else.

"He was really angry—and said just to have an abortion. Gookum said to come back—but not the baby. She said she was too old to have a baby crying in the house."

It hurt Lewis to hear the cold, hard facts. He'd been her third choice. Starla would have stayed with the baby's father—or with her grandma.

But he couldn't indulge his own feelings—not after all she'd been through. He took her hand and she didn't pull away.

"I'm glad they said no," he said tenderly. "Otherwise, I might not have had a chance to marry you. And I would have missed out on being Karissa's daddy."

She nodded and a couple of tears fell. But she didn't look back at him as she continued bravely on. "I didn't at first understand that my Grandma was involved at all. But when my father came for a visit, she'd always say that she'd leave us alone to have some special time together because it was my birthday or Christmas or whatever. She'd leave us alone in the house together."

"Maybe she didn't know what—what happened during those times," Missy suggested.

Lewis knew what people in the community thought—that Yvonne Quill was a wonderful woman for taking care of two small children at her age—raising them practically from birth—Garby hadn't been great at picking mothers for either of his children. And Yvonne was still taking care of the younger one—a 10-year-old boy.

"She knew," Starla said with a new sharpness in her tone. And Lewis saw a flash of anger in her eyes.

Maybe it was good that she was angry.

"I didn't realize it at first—when I was younger," Starla continued in a tightly controlled voice. "But as I grew older, I understood more of her comments and she grew bolder with them, too. She'd talk about the bed being wrinkled and stuff like that. And she started to call me names when she was mad at me. She'd call me a 'whore' or a 'prostitute' especially if I fixed my hair or wore something nice. She'd always be really mean to me for a week or two after my father left. And she'd make me show her what he'd given me. And she'd ask me if it was worth it—"

"How did the dresses come to be in her possession?" Keegan interjected.

Starla looked over at him in surprise, as if she'd forgotten he was even there. Then in answer to his question, she bowed her head and her voice was filled with shame. "I tried to destroy them."

"I wish I had been there to help you." Lewis felt a surge of grief and his voice broke. "I'd have ripped them to shreds—and thrown them in the fire."

Starla looked up at him in wonder. "That's what I was trying to do." She shook her head, remembering. "Gookum got *so angry!* She just kept hitting me and hitting me. And saying what a terrible daughter I was to destroy the expensive gifts my father had bought for me. And she made me always give her the things my father had given me right away. She said she couldn't trust me and she'd put them away until I was older and had the sense to take care of them."

Lewis felt rage sweep over him again. He wished he could hit the old woman—make her suffer the way that Starla had.

But Keegan's calm voice broke through his thoughts. "You said 'things' Starla. We were only looking for clothes. Did your father give you other 'gifts'?"

Lewis stared at his brother. With his uniform on and his notebook open, he had the stern look of a police officer conducting an investigation. This was the way to obtain justice—not with his fists. Lewis knew that.

"Yes," Starla answered.

Lewis turned wide eyes towards his wife. "There was more?"

he whispered.

Starla shrugged, but the tears in her eyes betrayed her true feelings. "Earrings and necklaces, shoes, makeup…"

Lewis glanced back at Keegan. He was writing everything down.

"We'll take a look for those things as well," he said. "As a matter of fact, I'll call right now. If Yvonne gets released, she might destroy some or all of it." He stood to his feet, walked a short distance away from them and made his call.

"I'm sorry," Joshua said in a voice thick with tears. "I didn't know."

Lewis was surprised at the gentleness in Starla's voice as she turned towards him. "You weren't that much older than me. And—he was hurting you, too. You were starting to tell me last night. Is that why he went to jail that time?"

"He's done this before!" Lewis exploded. "Why was he allowed back? Why wasn't he kept away from his children? Why didn't they keep him in jail?"

No one had an answer.

"When I was younger," Starla began again hesitantly, "sometimes the only thing I knew was that he was gone. Nobody ever told me why. And I never knew when he was coming back. But that time—when I was seven and went to live with my Gookum, I knew he had gone to jail. I just didn't know why."

"I wish the judge hadn't been so lenient," Joshua said. "They were tougher on Russell, our older brother."

"It didn't really seem to matter if he was in jail or not," Starla said. "He always somehow made it home for Christmas and for my birthday. I guess they felt sorry for him and let him come back for a day or two—to see his kids—and give us presents."

Her voice broke and Lewis drew her closer again.

But Starla still wanted to say something and she pulled away slightly to speak to Joshua. "You weren't able to help me then. But I owe it all to you now that I'm free and that my baby will never have to suffer. And—and that I don't have to leave Lewis. It's because of you. You made me tell my story. I didn't want to. You said that if I told someone else, I wouldn't be carrying the burden all alone." She looked around at them all. "And I'm not. Not anymore—and never again. I know that now."

She was actually smiling!

But Lewis wasn't at the point of rejoicing yet. He was still reeling from all the ugly, horrible things that she'd had to suffer throughout her life. He was still grieving for the childhood she'd never have. He was still angry at those who had hurt her—and those who hadn't helped her.

And he silently vowed that he would never leave her alone ever again. If she ran, he would run with her!

Keegan had been speaking quietly on the phone a little distance from them. He came back to join them. He looked carefully at Starla before speaking. "It would probably be best if you could identify the articles yourself…"

Lewis felt Starla shudder.

Keegan added quickly. "But I don't want to put you through any more right now. We're just going to take anything that we have any reason at all to suspect was involved with… the crimes. Colin's not sure they can hold Yvonne much longer. She's been charged and he's going to hold her there until we get done with her room." Keegan sighed. "I don't want to have to go through the process of forcing her to unlock it again."

Keegan looked tired. But then, they all were—especially Starla.

Lewis held her close as Keegan continued. "I was thinking that it might be best if you two left the community for a couple of days—till the dust settles a bit."

That sounded good to Lewis! But he had no idea where to go. Not Winnipeg—that was for sure!

"That's a great idea!" Joshua jumped to his feet. "You could take a vacation—a second honeymoon—get to know each other again."

Or for the first time.

Lewis looked cautiously down at Starla. "There was that hotel in Thunder Bay where we went last Christmas…"

Christmas… She'd been running from her father!

Joshua had gone somewhere while he was speaking. He came bounding back now, his face lit with excitement. "Here…" he said, holding a check out towards them.

Lewis felt Starla shrink back.

The smile left Joshua's face. "It's not for you," he said gently. "I'm giving it to Lewis. He can do with it what he wants."

Lewis took the piece of paper as Starla turned away. It was more money than Lewis made in a month. "Thanks," he said, feeling an overwhelming sense of gratitude.

"Your father gave you money as well?" Keegan asked quietly.

Starla merely nodded.

Keegan wrote something down.

"It's gone," Starla said. "She never wanted me to give her that. I spent it—to leave."

"It's another, separate conviction," Keegan told her, "if he gave you money."

Starla bowed her head.

"If you guys go," Joshua said, returning to the topic of the proposed trip, "I'd still like you to be back in time for our meeting Wednesday night."

Lewis lifted Starla's chin and looked into her eyes. "Would you like to go somewhere—together?" he asked softly.

She nodded and smiled tremulously.

"We could take care of Karissa," Missy offered.

"No!" Both Lewis and Starla spoke at once.

"Or not…" Missy laughed.

Lewis was embarrassed by their quick reaction and felt he needed to explain. "Maybe some other time. But for now, I think we both just want to keep her close."

"We understand," Joshua assured him.

"You'll need to pack some clothes," Keegan said practically. "But I'd like you both under police protection until you're on your way."

"It's Easter," Missy said. "There won't be any flights out today."

"I'll call Bill," Keegan said. "I'd really like you guys out of harm's way for a few days. If I explain the situation to him…" He stood to his feet and Joshua handed him the phone.

Keegan walked away from them as he dialed. They heard him greet Bill and then his voice faded.

Keegan was back a few minutes later. "Bill can be ready in about forty–five minutes. He'll meet us at the airport. I'll go with you over to your house and stay with you while you pack."

Lewis felt bad thinking about waking Karissa up after she'd just got settled in for the night but when Starla walked down the stairs, Karissa was still fast asleep on her shoulder. They slipped her jacket on, still without waking her—a major achievement!

It felt strange for Lewis to have her back in their house again. And it felt stranger yet that he was helping her pack. Only this time he was going with her.

But it must have felt strange for Starla, too. She stood looking down at the open drawer as if unable to decide what to leave and what to pack.

Lewis felt the same way. It was a new beginning—a fresh start.

"Joshua gave me a lot of money," Lewis began cautiously. "Enough for you to do a little shopping…"

She looked up then and smiled at him. And Lewis felt his heart leap into his throat.

She was so beautiful! And he loved her so much!

There had never been a lot of passion in their marriage. They had done what married people do but he knew now that she could just as easily have done it—and had—with a complete stranger. And he'd sensed, even before, that she hadn't been giving her whole self to him—just her body.

And he'd always been so nervous around her—afraid that he'd do or say something that would make her want to leave again.

But now there was a new connection between them—a new tenderness and a trust.

And part of Lewis wanted to give way to the passion he'd stored up for her for so long—to really show her how much he loved her!

But he knew that because of what had happened with her father, he needed to go very slowly—and always wait for her cues before going any further.

But… if she kept smiling at him like that!

And in that moment, she put her arms up around his neck and kissed him.

It wasn't like any other kiss they'd ever shared. It was a promise and it was an invitation and it was a commitment for a lifetime.

"Hey, are you guys about done…?"

Keegan's voice trailed off and he stepped quickly out again, shutting the door as he went.

They had sprung apart at the sound of his voice. But then they both looked at each other and started laughing.

Lewis couldn't ever remember having such freedom and this incredible feeling of reckless joy—as if he could conquer the world!

"So I guess you like the idea of shopping…" he teased.

Starla smiled. "Uh–huh." Then she looked down at the open drawer again. "But I do want to at least get some clean clothes for tomorrow. And we should pack something for Karissa, too."

"Actually," Lewis admitted, "I usually pack way too much for her. I think she still has several outfits left in her bag that we brought from the lodge. And I packed a bunch of her toys, too."

Tears sprang to Starla's eyes. "You're such a good daddy. I wish—I wish I could be a good mother."

Lewis wrapped his arms around her. "You're going to be," he assured her. "And you already are." He pulled away a little to look into her eyes. "You were ready to risk everything to protect your daughter. She's very lucky to have you. You're a great mom. And she loves you. She missed you so much when you were gone. We both did."

She was getting that tender look in her eyes again—love *for him!*

"C'mon," he laughed. "If we don't get out of here pretty soon, Keegan's really going to be suspecting that we're up to something."

Starla gave him a quick kiss on the cheek and threw a few things into a bag. "Well, I'm done," she declared. "How about you?"

"I think I still have enough stuff packed, too," he said, glancing down at the packsack that had been to Winnipeg and back. "We'll need our coats, though."

Starla picked up the two bags in one hand and grabbed his arm with the other. "C'mon, let's go!"

She sounded happier and more excited than he'd ever heard her before.

"All right, all right!" Lewis laughed as he allowed her to pull him out of the bedroom towards the front door. She grabbed his coat and helped him put it on then slipped on hers as well.

Karissa was still asleep on the couch where they'd laid her. Keegan took their bags while Starla carefully picked up their daughter and carried her out.

Chapter 13

LEWIS AND STARLA COULD EASILY have spent the whole day in their hotel room but by mid–afternoon, Karissa was tired of playing with the few toys they'd brought and bored with the cartoons on TV. She'd had a short nap but seemed full of energy—too much energy for a small hotel room!

Their hotel had a pool so they decided to make use of that. Lewis opted to sit on a deckchair and watch Starla and Karissa play, his heart filled to overflowing with love for the both of them.

By Tuesday, Lewis felt ready to venture out to the mall, being able finally to walk without groaning every step of the way! He still had to take it a bit slow but Karissa preferred to walk rather than be held so this kept their pace pretty slow anyway.

They stopped first at a children's clothing store where Starla and Lewis bought Karissa a cute little outfit, a new spring coat, and some splash boots. Then they went to a toy store, remembering to keep their purchases small so they would be easier to bring home on the plane. They bought a little wooden puzzle and some hardcover books but what Karissa was really drawn to were the pull–toys. They ended up buying her a little wooden doggy that when pulled, wagged its floppy ears and tail.

It quickly become Karissa's favorite toy and she pulled it along behind her everywhere she went.

Lewis knew where he wanted to go next and he steered his little family towards a jewelry store that he'd been to once before. Just as they arrived there, the string on Karissa's pull–toy got tangled on one of the wheels. Starla bent down to fix it, kissed Karissa on the cheek then straightened up and looked around.

Her face went pale and Lewis was afraid for a moment that she might faint or something. He quickly put his arms around her.

"Did you think I wouldn't notice?" he asked gently.

"Lewis…"

She was going to cry. And he wasn't about to let that happen. "C'mon," he teased, pulling on her arm. "That saleslady over there's looking like she's ready to throw me out. If you start crying, she'll think I beat you or something and I'll be turfed out of here for sure!"

Starla's eyes grew wide. "But you've never, ever hit me!"

Lewis laughed and pulled her closer to the ring counter. "C'mon," he said, "let's spend some money before we both get thrown out."

The saleslady *was* looking a little askance at them. But as soon as Lewis began to point out some expensive rings, her manner changed completely.

It was Starla that whispered, "Can we afford these?" when the woman had bent down to take out another tray for them to look at.

"Yes," he assured her, "I was able to save a bit of money…" He almost said *while you were gone* but stopped himself. The saleslady was distracting them now anyway, showing them beautiful engagement and wedding bands.

Lewis hadn't spent very much of either of his paychecks this past month while she'd been gone. People were always bringing food over to him—and they'd eaten up at the camp quite a bit, too. There was no mortgage on their house and he used wood heat. And he hadn't been doing any more renovations...

"I like this one," Starla said shyly, moving her hand towards Lewis so he could see better.

"It's beautiful," he said glancing at the ring briefly before looking up into her eyes again. *You're the one who's beautiful* he longed to say.

"Would you like the men's band?" The saleslady's voice broke off as she saw the ring on Lewis's finger.

He smiled at her. "We've been married for a while. My wife just lost her wedding band."

She smiled kindly at them. "I would have guessed you two were just recently engaged or perhaps newlyweds. Except, of course," she quickly amended, "for your cute little daughter there."

"Doggy!" Karissa spoke as if on cue.

Lewis bent down beside her. "That's right, honey. It's a 'doggy'."

"Doggy! Doggy! Doggy!"

Lewis laughed as he straightened up again. He caught the saleslady's words, "...such a good father," and heard Starla reply, "Yes, he is."

But she was getting teary–eyed again. Lewis gently squeezed her hand and smiled at her. Starla quickly wiped away the tears and Lewis lifted her other hand up, glanced at the ring and said, "Okay, we'll buy this one."

The saleslady smiled at them and said, "I think you're probably a size 6."

"Maybe a 5," Lewis suggested.

The woman measured Starla's finger and looked up at him in

surprise.

"A size 5," she said. "Most men wouldn't know things like that."

Most men wouldn't have bought three wedding bands in less than two years.

Lewis shook his thoughts free. He needed to think about their future now.

"Can I wear it right away?" Starla asked.

"Of course, dear," the woman said. "Just hang onto your receipt."

Lewis paid using his bankcard and a moment later they were out of the store and walking towards one of the mall exits.

Starla put out her hand to stop him.

He looked at her inquiringly.

"I'll never take it off," she said, "not ever."

And he knew she really meant it. She had spoken the words like a vow—a wedding vow.

He kissed her then, right there in the middle of the mall! But to him, it was a sacred place and a sacred moment—a renewal of their wedding vows.

It wasn't a long kiss but still someone walking by called out, "Hey, buddy, get a room!"

Starla flushed with embarrassment but Lewis just laughed. "Sounds like a good idea to me!"

THEY TOOK THE LAST FLIGHT out on Wednesday, arriving back just minutes before the meeting that they'd promised Joshua they would attend.

They had called ahead, letting Joshua know what time their plane was coming in. Lewis was a little surprised that he was the only one there to meet them but he thought maybe Keegan was working or that everyone was up at the lodge ready and waiting for them to start the meeting.

He was further surprised when Joshua drove them over to the Community Center instead. There weren't any other cars around but Lewis thought maybe the others had walked.

"We're having the meeting here instead?" Starla asked, echoing Lewis's thoughts.

But Joshua only made some small noise in his throat that didn't really sound like a yes or a no. He insisted upon carrying Karissa and as they walked up the steps, he said, "You mentioned yesterday that you'd bought a new ring for Starla…"

"Yes," Lewis said, looking quickly at Starla. He hoped she wasn't upset that he'd told Joshua.

But she was smiling shyly at him and Lewis got lost for a moment, just thinking about how beautiful she was and how much he loved her…

"A'hem!"

Lewis tore his eyes away from Starla and glanced sheepishly at Joshua who was grinning from ear to ear.

"I guess Missy was right," he said.

"About what?" Lewis asked.

"Doggy! Doggy!" Karissa joined in the conversation, waving her favorite toy so Joshua could see.

And then Missy herself was at the door, waving them in.

"Surprise!"

Joshua looked around the room. It looked as if half the community was there! For sure, everyone from their church was. And they were all smiling and yelling "surprise" and coming over to hug them!

Missy grabbed a microphone and quieted everyone down.

"I guess all of you know why we're here." She looked over at Starla and Lewis. "With the possible exception of these two."

Everyone laughed and Lewis glanced quickly at Starla. She was looking as confused as he was but at least she was smiling and seemed ready to hear the rest of what Missy had to say.

"We've had some dark days around here," Missy continued in a quieter voice. "But the Lord has been very good. And he's brought two people back together who should never have been apart."

Starla slipped her hand into his and Lewis smiled at her as she turned shining eyes towards him.

"We think," Missy continued softly, "that this is cause for celebration."

Keegan took a turn at the microphone then. "We didn't have a chance to give you a big party at your wedding…" he began.

Lewis nodded, remembering the difficult time it had been for Keegan and Randi. She'd had a miscarriage just days before Starla and Lewis's wedding. They'd still gone ahead with it but there had only been a few people there and a quiet gathering in their home afterwards. Neither Starla's father nor her Aunt Yvonne had attended and there'd been a big fight with them when Lewis helped Starla move her things over to his house that afternoon. Garby and Yvonne had both been drunk and there'd been a lot of yelling and cursing. Not the best wedding night.

"We kinda wanted to make it up to you now," Keegan continued, putting an arm around Randi who was standing beside him. "And we heard you'd even bought new rings…"

Lewis was about to correct him and say they'd only bought one but Starla was smiling and holding up her hand for people to see. Everyone clapped and cheered.

Keegan raised a hand for silence again. "Sometimes when married people are apart and come together again, they have what's called a renewal of vows."

Keegan stepped aside and the pastor of their church came to the microphone.

"If you'd like…" Pastor Thomas said gently, smiling at Starla and Lewis.

Lewis knew without even looking at her. She was squeezing his hand and he could sense her happiness and excitement. It wasn't something he would have thought of on his own. But he was happy to do it for her.

They stepped forward, Missy pressed a small bouquet of daisies into Starla's hands and the pastor directed them to stand in front of him. He smiled and looked out over the crowd standing informally around them. "We are gathered here today to witness the *re*union of Starla and Lewis Littledeer in Holy Matrimony. This is a solemn occasion…"

No, Lewis thought, *this is a joyous occasion!* He could barely keep from whooping out loud as the pastor continued.

The words flowed over and around them, reaffirming their love and commitment to one another.

They both said "I do" at the appropriate times and Lewis was happy to oblige when asked to kiss the bride!

Another roar of applause rose up around them and then there were more hugs and more words of congratulations.

Then Joshua announced that the "bride and groom" needed to cut the cake. Lewis and Starla walked over to a big table laden down with gifts of all shapes and sizes, some wrapped with paper and some with just a ribbon around them and some with just a little note pinned on.

But in the middle of the table, there was a beautiful white three–tier wedding cake with a little ceramic teddy bear bride and groom on top! Jamie Martin, the wife of pilot, Bill Martin, was standing beside it holding a cake knife with a white ribbon tied onto it.

Lewis and Starla both stood speechless with amazement.

"I still had everything from Rosalee's wedding," Jamie explained, referring to her daughter who had been married just a few months earlier. "It didn't take long for me to make the cake."

"It's beautiful," Starla said softly.

Lewis and Starla stood behind the cake and several people snapped pictures as they held hands and made the first cut in the bottom layer of the cake.

Lewis and Starla served cake to everyone, receiving once again the congratulations and best wishes of each person gathered.

There was lots of other food as well and people were encouraged to help themselves from the large assortment of dishes on the tables set up against the wall.

Lewis finally got a chance to thank Missy and Joshua. It had been a wonderful thing for them to do, not just for them as a couple but for Starla and the community as well. People had always been quite supportive of Lewis but a lot of people had felt quite differently about Starla. Word must have spread quickly after Garby was arrested because everyone was very sympathetic towards her now. Several people, including former schoolteachers and people in the church, apologized to her for not investigating more closely some of the suspicions that they'd had while she was growing up.

It made Lewis angry to hear them but Starla was so gracious and forgiving that he felt he had no right to be angry on her behalf.

And it was a new beginning—for all of them.

Lewis just hoped that people had learned something and that

they would all be more aware in the future. He didn't want to think that there might be other little girls or boys out there being sexually abused. But he hated the idea even more that it might be happening and no one was noticing. Starla's experiences were a lesson for them all.

It was a strange mix of emotions for him, thinking about the past and the future. But Starla seemed to be feeling nothing but happiness as she smiled and talked and laughed, and gave and received hugs.

And Karissa was in her element as well. People were showering her with attention and complimenting her on how beautiful and how smart she was. Karissa chattered happily with each person and got cake all over her hands, face and clothes. Starla washed her off as best she could but then someone else gave her something to eat and she was soon covered in sticky goo once more! And Missy was snapping pictures of everyone...

Some of the families with younger children started to leave around nine o'clock. Karissa had fallen asleep in Missy's arms by that time. Lewis and Starla had made their way around to everyone and people were starting to gather up dishes and tidy up the hall.

Joshua offered to drive them home whenever they were ready and both Lewis and Starla agreed that they were ready now.

As they walked through the front door, Lewis did almost feel as if he was bringing his new bride home for the first time. They had both changed so much in the last few days and they had grown so much together. Lewis now understood what it felt like to be one—together not just in body but in soul and in spirit.

Joshua and Starla carried their gifts and luggage in while Lewis got Karissa ready for bed. She woke up a little but went right back to sleep again.

When Lewis walked out to join them, Joshua was already gone and their living room seemed filled to overflowing with the gifts from their reception and with the clothes and toys they had bought in Thunder Bay.

Lewis thought that Starla would want to open some of the gifts right away but she seemed quiet and even a little sad.

He walked quickly to where she stood and put his arms around her. "What's the matter?" he asked gently.

She was staring at all the gifts and there were tears in her eyes. "I don't deserve all this," she whispered. "Just because I came back… It was wrong for me to leave in the first place. I shouldn't be given a party and gifts for doing something wrong."

Lewis just hugged her for a moment. Then he cleared a spot on the couch and pulled her down beside him. "First off," he said, kissing her gently on the forehead, "this party wasn't just for you. It was for *us*. It was a celebration of our marriage and our new life together and an opportunity for people to rejoice about what the Lord has done for both of us—and for Karissa."

"Secondly," Lewis said, "did you ever hear the story of the 'prodigal son'? Now, there was a guy who really blew it. And his father threw him a humungous party when he finally arrived back home again."

Starla looked up at him and smiled faintly. "Yeah, that's kind of how I feel, I guess. I really blew it and everybody threw us a party and gave us presents and everything."

"It's a pretty good picture of how God feels too," Lewis said gently. "We all blow it—on a regular basis—and He always takes us back—every time."

"It's that love thing again, isn't it?"

Lewis laughed. "Yeah, it's that love thing."

Chapter 14

IN THE END, STARLA WAS glad that they'd waited until the next morning before opening any of their gifts because Karissa had so much fun with the wrapping paper and the ribbons. And there were a few new toys included in the gifts for her as well.

Joshua called just before lunch to tell them that the support group meeting that they'd been planning for the night before, would instead be held that evening. And Missy arrived later that afternoon with a binder of material for Starla to read over in preparation for the meeting.

It all felt very overwhelming to Starla. She wished that she could just forget about it all—pretend none of that stuff with her father had ever happened. But one day in the future she knew there would be a trial and she would be required to give testimony...

After Missy left, Lewis, still recovering from his injuries, laid down for a nap with Karissa, and Starla was left alone with her thoughts.

It felt strange to be back in their house again and stranger still to be awake while they both slept. It somehow made her feel like an outsider again. But Starla reminded herself—that wasn't the way that Lewis and Karrisa thought of her.

It didn't help that there was a picture up on the wall of just the two of them. It was a beautiful picture that someone had taken of Karissa and Lewis walking hand in hand down a tree–lined path. They had their backs turned from the person taking the picture and it looked so sweet and so sad too. Starla wished that she was holding Karissa's other hand in the picture.

Suddenly, she wondered if she had any pictures at all of her and Karissa together.

Starla got up and found the box of photographs that Lewis kept on a shelf in the kitchen. She brought the box over and sat down on the couch to look through it. She'd never bothered much with pictures; Lewis was the one who liked them. He always had a little camera up on top of the refrigerator and he'd run and get it sometimes, usually if Karissa was doing something cute or had learned some wonderful new skill.

Starla saw that in the front of the box, there were a few more of Lewis and Karissa. Starla thought that Missy had probably taken them. She loved taking pictures and was always snapping her camera at someone.

There were more of Karissa alone and some of Lewis doing various carpentry projects, all from the winter before. Starla remembered Lewis showing her some of them. He was always so excited when he got some pictures developed, he'd usually go around showing everyone!

Starla kept on looking through the pictures. So far, she hadn't found a single one of her and Karissa together. She'd found one of her alone, waving away the camera when they were unwrapping gifts in Thunder Bay the Christmas before.

The pictures were lined up in the box between cardboard dividers that told what month they were taken. But as Starla kept looking further back, she found a bulging envelope that took her by surprise. It was labeled: "For Starla."

Cautiously, she opened it, wondering why Lewis had never told her that it was there. But maybe he had mentioned once that he had some pictures to show her and she'd brushed him off.

Starla looked through the envelope and realized that they were all pictures of Karissa taken during the seven months when Starla had been away the previous time. They were neatly labeled with how old Karissa was and sometimes Lewis had also written things about the picture like: "Karissa's first tooth!" "Karissa rolled over today—Jan 23!" "Karissa sitting up by herself!" "Karissa playing drums with daddy."

By the time Starla looked through them all, she was weeping. *She'd missed so much!* But Lewis—faithful Lewis—had taken the time to record it all and keep it for her.

"Hey, what's the matter?"

She'd been so intent on looking at the pictures that she hadn't heard him coming out of the bedroom.

He sat down and put his arm around her. "You found the pictures…"

Starla's eyes filled with tears. "You never told me about them."

Lewis turned away. "I think I mentioned them once or twice. You never seemed very interested."

"I'm sorry," Starla said quickly and Lewis turned towards her again as she continued. "I should have wanted to see the pictures. I guess it was just that I didn't want to have to think about how much I'd missed."

"Thank you for taking all these pictures," Starla said sincerely.

Lewis relaxed and smiled at her. "You're welcome," he said.

Then as she slid the baby pictures of Karissa back into the envelope, he asked, "Were you looking for anything in particular?"

"I…" Starla looked down. Did she even have a right to ask? She'd been gone for so much of Karissa's young life.

"What is it?" Lewis asked gently.

"I was looking for a picture of Karissa and me," Starla said hesitantly.

Lewis slid the box over onto his lap. "Well, there must be some."

"No, I don't think so."

Lewis flipped through them anyway.

But there wasn't any. Not even newborn pictures. It had been a difficult delivery and they had both been exhausted. And Karissa had been a fussy baby and even Lewis hadn't taken many pictures those first days and weeks.

And there hadn't been any grandparents "oohing" and "aahing" over the new baby and taking pictures either.

Lewis stood up. "We can fix that, you know."

He went and got his camera from off the top of the fridge.

"Karissa's asleep and my eyes are all red from crying," Starla protested.

Lewis wagged a finger at her. "Okay, but I'm not taking no for an answer next time. In the next day or two, for sure, okay?"

Starla smiled up at him. "Okay."

Lewis slipped the camera into his sweatshirt pocket and sat down beside her again. "So did you get a chance to look through the stuff for support group tonight?" he asked.

Starla had glanced through it once when Missy had first brought it over. "Not really," she replied. "To tell you the truth, I really wish we weren't going. I'm not sure I'm ready for all this yet."

Lewis put his arm around her. "I know," he said sympathetically. "I don't really feel like I'm ready either. But I know it's the right thing to do."

Starla sighed. "Yeah, I guess I know that, too."

"Maybe we could do our homework together," he suggested.

She laughingly agreed. "I feel like I'm a kid in school again—*homework!*"

Lewis brought the two binders of material over and handed one to her.

They opened them up together and found the homework questions for that week. As she read through it, Starla groaned in despair. "*More pictures!*"

Lewis said thoughtfully, "I'm not sure that I have any pictures of myself as a kid."

"I *know* I don't!" Starla exclaimed in an exasperated voice.

"It does say we can draw a picture of ourselves if we don't have any."

Starla slammed the book shut. "I don't know how to draw."

Lewis pulled her book onto his lap and handed her his. "Tell you what," he said with a grin. "I'll draw you and you draw me."

Starla laughed and wrinkled her nose. "You were a real skinny little kid."

"Yeah," Lewis retorted, "and you were a big tomboy always waiting to beat me up."

Her eyes widened. "I was not!"

"Yeah, you were! Remember that time you pushed me off the dock right after breakup. There were still big chunks of ice on the lake."

"Actually, I do remember that," Starla said. "Keegan was so mad at me. I really thought he was going to throw me in, too!"

"And I told him that you didn't know how to swim."

"Yeah," Starla said softly. "I remember you sticking up for me.

I was kind of surprised."

Lewis grinned. "Guess I sort of had a crush on you even then."

"Well, I guess I could try to draw a picture of you," Starla conceded. "But you'd better not laugh at it!"

"I won't, I promise."

Lewis found a couple of pencils in one of the kitchen drawers and they both sat down at the table and began to draw.

Lewis was done almost right away but Starla was taking her time. "I remember you had kinda spiky hair," she mused, as she continued drawing. "And you always looked a little sad. You never smiled very much." She drew his eyes looking straight ahead, expressionless. His chin was tilted down a little. It was as she remembered him, a small, quiet boy with the weight of the world on his shoulders.

"Wow!"

Starla heard the admiration in his voice and glanced shyly up at him.

"I thought you said you didn't know how to draw!" he exclaimed.

"Well, I don't," she insisted.

"Uh–hum, so why do I want to take this little boy home and give him all the love and security he's been missing all his life?"

Starla smiled and kept drawing, adding some finishing touches.

"You've managed to put so much expression in his face," Lewis continued. "It's amazing. Where did you ever learn to draw so well?"

"Well… I did take art one year in high school but I failed the course."

"*You failed!* Was your teacher blind?"

"No, I just didn't hand in most of my assignments. I never

thought they were good enough."

Lewis put his arm around her. "Starla, you are very talented! And I want you to keep drawing, okay? And whatever you want to buy—paintbrushes or special pencils or paper or whatever—you do that. We'll look for a place to buy them on the Internet and look in art stores when we go to the city."

Starla felt more embarrassed than ever but she was pleased, too.

"Ready to do the rest of the homework?" he asked.

But drawing the picture was the easy part.

Answering the questions was more difficult than she could ever have imagined.

"Don't think too much," Lewis advised. "Just go through it quick and check off the ones you think apply to you."

She took his advice and moved quickly through the two pages, trying hard not to think about having to report her answers in a group discussion.

THEY HAD ARRANGED FOR A babysitter, Jamie and Bill's youngest daughter, sixteen-year-old Kaitlyn, to take care of Chance and Karissa up in the nursery.

Starla got Karissa settled in and then came down to join the group already assembled around the table with binders open.

Missy had told her who would be there and Starla felt comfortable with most of the group. Keegan, Randi, Joshua, Missy, and of course, Lewis, were all familiar to her. The only person she didn't know very well was Jasmine.

Jasmine, Missy's half-sister, had Missy's curly hair and wide smile but that was where the similarities ended. It was obvious that both of Jasmine's parents were white, and at least one of Missy's parents was black. Jasmine was also carrying at least twenty extra pounds of weight while Missy was slim with just a little "baby bump" this far along in her pregnancy.

Starla felt uncomfortable thinking about sharing her deepest feelings with a complete stranger in the room. She felt even more uncomfortable when Jasmine began the sharing time by saying that she couldn't do the homework because she'd had a really good childhood.

Starla felt angry. *What was she even doing here—just gloating?*

But Jasmine noticed her reaction and added quickly, "I shared with the others last week." Her voice dropped to a little above a whisper. "I was raped just a little over nine months ago. I just gave birth to the twin girls that resulted from the rape." Tears filled her eyes. "They're beautiful—and I can't imagine my life now without them. But…"

She hesitated and looked around the group. "I know I haven't suffered nearly as much as many of you have."

"We're not into comparing or competing here," Joshua said. "It's impossible to measure one person's pain as compared to another's. And Jasmine, I hope you know you're welcome here."

"Thanks," she said softly. "Last week really helped me a lot and I was looking ahead in the materials and I think some of the other lessons will be good, too."

Joshua nodded, looking around at the group. "Not all of the information or questions in all of our lessons will apply to everyone each time. All of us just need to remember to be open to the Lord for what He has to teach us for that week."

He had already mentioned the issue of confidentiality and asked Starla to sign a sheet that they'd all signed the week before.

Now he brought up another point. "It's important," he said, addressing the whole group, "that when you're telling your story, you don't victimize others in the group by using graphic physical details to describe what happened to you. What you need to be working through is your own thoughts and feelings about the abuse—how it affected you then and now."

He flipped over a page in his notebook and Starla could see that he too had drawn a picture on his homework sheet. She looked around the group and found that all the others, except her and Lewis, had photographs.

Keegan looked apologetically over at Lewis's page. "I think I have a picture or two of you. When we cleaned out mom and dad's room—after the funeral—there was a bunch of stuff. I just put it all in a box. Randi and I went through some of it today."

Starla reached out and squeezed Lewis's hand knowing it was hard for him to hear what Keegan was saying.

"Maybe you and Starla could come over some time and we could look through the box together. There are a couple of pictures you might like to have."

Lewis nodded solemnly. Then he smiled. "You guys won't believe the awesome picture Starla drew of me."

He showed the picture around to everyone and Starla was embarrassed all over again by their exclamations of surprise and their effusive praise.

"Oh, that reminds me," Missy said. "I have some pictures from last night for you guys."

"Already?" Lewis exclaimed.

"Yeah, I did them up on the computer," Missy said. "There's a really awesome one of Starla and Karissa. I can blow it up for you if you like."

Starla and Lewis exchanged smiles and Lewis said softly, "Yeah, we'd really like that a lot."

"Well, maybe we should continue," Joshua said. "Missy, why don't you go next?"

Missy smiled at everyone and began. "Jasmine is my sister… Even though we look nothing like each other. We had the same mother but her father adopted me so we're only technically half–sisters. But I had a great childhood. I was well loved by my mother and my adoptive father. And I had an awesome Grandma and Grandpa. But Joshua and I were talking and I know that there are still some things that maybe I need to deal with, too.

"Being blind was not too bad in the safety of my parent's house but it was a lot harder out in the community. And I guess another thing that I didn't fully realize until I could see was why people sometimes treated me different. It's kind of funny, I guess, but I didn't really understand about being a different color than everyone else around me. I mean, I knew I was partly of African–American descent but it didn't really hit home till I could actually see the difference in skin color between me and Joshua, and between me and my sister. And when I was blind, I wasn't able to see people's expressions when they were looking at me. Now, it's all a little bit clearer—and a little bit more painful." She looked down at her homework sheet. "But I guess I have to say that my case is similar to Jasmine's and these questions don't really apply to me either."

Joshua smiled at her and said, "Thanks," before turning an inquiring eye towards Keegan. "Would you mind going next?"

Keegan talked about his experiences of being verbally and physically abused and as he shared his story, Starla realized that like Jasmine and Missy, the two brothers Keegan and Lewis, had a lot in common.

Randi shared next. Starla knew that she had been raised by a single mother who had died of alcohol–related complications when Randi was eleven. After that, she had been in a series of foster homes. But what Randi had to share was not about her past but about her present and future. "I'm pregnant," she announced to the group. The slight tremor in her voice and the way that she clutched Keegan's hand produced cautious congratulations from the group. "I shouldn't be," she said with a fragile smile. "I thought I wouldn't get pregnant so soon after having Chance, especially since I was nursing him."

"How far along are you?" Missy asked gently.

Randi bowed her head. "About four months."

Missy smiled broadly. "So you'll have your baby a couple of months ahead of me."

But her words obviously meant to cheer, had the opposite effect.

"If—if I have—" Randi's voice broke and tears filled her eyes. Keegan put his arm around her and drew her close.

After a moment, he glanced around the group, saw the question in Jasmine's eyes and explained. "Randi had two miscarriages before Chance was born. We're afraid…" His voice trailed off.

Joshua led the group in prayer for them and for their unborn child.

There was a moment of silence then it was Starla's turn to share.

She found it unexpectedly difficult to actually say the words, "this child was sexually abused," even though most of those gathered around the table already knew. She was glad that the homework sheets had at least allowed her to distance herself a little and not have to use the pronoun "I" but even as she continued to talk about "this child," her voice shook a little as she admitted that she felt it would have been better if she had never been born. And when it came to the last question, she wept openly as she said she wished she could adopt that child and hold her as long as she wanted to be held.

"I'll hold you," Lewis said.

He moved his chair closer and put his arm around her and held her hand. Starla smiled up at him, feeling a well of love springing up in her heart.

"Now I know you two are just newlyweds…" Joshua teased.

Lewis and Starla tore their eyes away from each other and turned towards the rest of the group. Everyone was smiling at them.

"Lewis, would you like to share next?" Joshua asked after a moment.

Starla felt him withdraw a little away from her.

The healing journey was, in its very essence, a solitary one.

"I guess maybe Keegan got the brunt of the physical and verbal abuse," Lewis began. "What I felt most—and what I most struggle with now—is being abandoned.

"I think I felt that most from my mother. I tried—" His voice broke. "I tried so hard! But nothing—*nothing*—helped. She—she left me, anyways."

"Lewis, that wasn't your fault," Keegan protested.

Lewis raised tear–filled eyes to look at his brother. "A part of me knows that, I guess," he said. "But maybe it's the difference between my head and my heart. I still *feel* as if I let her down somehow."

"And you feel as if she abandoned you," Joshua said.

"Yeah, I do." Lewis lowered his eyes again. "And I always feel as if maybe there's something more I can do or someone else that I should be—stronger or bigger or tougher."

"You feel that way even now?" Joshua asked.

Lewis nodded. "When Starla leaves—or even when I just think about her leaving—or dream about it—I think maybe I panic and make things worse. Maybe I try too hard."

Starla felt as if her heart had stopped beating. She'd hurt this man who she loved—this man who loved her—*she'd hurt him so much!*

He had drawn away from her. Now it was her turn to reach out to him. She put her arm around him and told hold of his hand. "Lewis, it's nothing you've done," she said softly. "It was my fault—and my dad's fault. You are the most awesome guy I know. You're a great husband and a really great father and I promise…"

She waited until he looked up at her then with all the love she felt for him, she said, "I promise you, Lewis Littledeer, that I will never leave you again."

They both had tears in their eyes as they embraced.

Joshua asked if they could pray as a group for them.

Starla and Lewis both nodded as the others came to stand around them.

Each of them prayed for Starla and Lewis and for Karissa as well. Lewis prayed, too and finally Starla prayed as well, asking for the Lord to bless their marriage and their family.

There were more hugs and more teary–eyed smiles.

And then it was time to go home… home with Lewis… her husband… her best friend.

Author's Note

If you have been sexually abused, it is very important that you talk to someone you trust: a teacher or your pastor or youth counselor.

If you know of someone under the age of sixteen who is being sexually abused, it is against the law to not report it to the authorities: the police or a social agency.

If you have been sexually abused in the past, the first step on your journey of healing will be to acknowledge that it happened and that it is affecting you today. You need to look honestly at the problems in your life and be willing to accept the help and counsel of others.

To know Jesus is to know the Great Healer. The Bible says that God loves you. He loves you so much that He sent Jesus to pay the price for your sin (it's like somebody taking your jail sentence for you so you can go free). Speaking of Himself in John 10:10 and 11, Jesus said: "I came that they might have life, a great full life. I am the Good Shepherd. The Good Shepherd gives His life for the sheep."

Jesus gave His life for you. But the Good News is that He didn't stay dead. He came alive again after three days. The Bible says that He "swallowed up death in victory"! (Isaiah 25:8 and I Corinthians 15:54 KJV).

He only asks us to trust Him. A simple but often difficult decision for someone who has been betrayed by those whom they should have been able to trust. Though your earthly father may have hurt you, your Heavenly Father loves you and because He is perfect, His love for you is perfect.

Life here on earth may be difficult but it is a journey we all must take. There is Someone who wants to walk beside us. When we talk to God and tell Him of our troubles, He hears us and the Bible says that the Holy Spirit is there to comfort us. As you read more of the Bible, you will learn more about God and He will speak truth to your mind and to your heart.

The Lord bless you!

M. Dorene Meyer
dorene@dorenemeyer.com

Recommended Resources

1. The Bible—available in many versions. Find one that's easy for you to read.
2. Visit www.risingabove.ca—excellent site that will direct you towards resources, conferences in your area, and hope and healing.
3. *Hope for the Hurting,* by Howard Jolly, published by Rising Above Counseling Agency in 1996.
4. *How to Counsel a Sexually Abused Person,* by Selma Poulin, also published by Rising Above Counseling Agency.
5. *Helping Victims of Sexual Abuse,* by Lynn Heitritter and Jeanette Vought, published by Bethany House Publishers in 1989.
6. *A Door of Hope,* by Jan Frank, published by Thomas Nelson Publishers in 1993.
7. *Breaking the Silence*, by Rose–Aimee Bordeleau, published by Raphah Worldwide Ministries in 2002, and available from www.raphah.org.

Questions for Group Discussion or Personal Reflection— Week Two

For your homework this week, attach a photo of yourself as a child here: (If you do not own or cannot obtain a picture, draw a picture of yourself as a child.)

Answer the following questions about the child in the photo. **You may share all or just some of your answers with the group, as you feel comfortable:** (both genders are used because abuse happens to boys and girls both)

1. This child was

    - sexually abused ____
    - physically abused ____
    - verbally abused ____
    - abandoned ____

2. This child was abused because:

    - she was born ____
    - he had sick parents who took out their misery on him and got away with it because nobody cared ____
    - of her need to be nurtured by a father figure ____
    - because she developed too soon ____
    - because she didn't say no ____
    - because he was there and he was small ____

3. This child needed:

    - to be still–born ____
    - to be born to other parents ____
    - to be taken out of the home ____
    - someone to listen to her ____
    - to have someone care about him and help him ____
    - love and attention from her dad ____
    - she really needed her mom ____

4. This child felt:

    - powerless ____
    - momentary satisfaction and acceptance from someone he thought really cared____
    - feelings of guilt for allowing the abuse to happen____
    - that she deserved her treatment because she wasn't worthy of anything better ____
    - that life will never change____
    - confused, abandoned, rejected, alone ____

5. This child believed:

    - that something was wrong with her, that she was bad ____
    - that sexual feelings were bad and to be kept secret ____
    - it was okay to be abused as long as it made Dad happy ____
    - that it was an acceptable way to show love ____
    - that she was unloved, despised and worthy of ugly, abusive treatment ____
    - that if he told anyone, he would get into a lot of trouble ____

6. This child decided:

    - to withdraw and put up a front to be whatever those around her wanted her to be ____
    - to play along and hide what she was really feeling ____
    - that no one could be trusted and everyone was out to hurt him ____
    - to just be quiet and forget about it ____

7. If I were to adopt this child, l would:
    - show the child more love in a nurturing, non–sexual way, because otherwise the child will look for acceptance in a sexual way ____
    - help him to feel loved and safe about talking about his feelings because he is a special person and very gifted ____
    - not do it because she has wounds and scars that are too deep to heal. The best I could do is leave her alone and not hurt her anymore ____
    - hold her as long as she wanted to be held and give her lots of hugs ____

The above lesson was adapted from pages 153–156 of "Helping Victims of Sexual Abuse" by Lynn Heitritter and Jeanette Vought, Bethany House Publishers, 1989.